Cinnamon Kisses & Forever Wishes

THE THATCHER BROTHERS OF ACORN FIELD HEIGHTS
BOOK TWO

MAGGIE ELLIS

Also by Maggie Ellis

STANDALONES

The Christmas Cabin Mix-Up

THE THATCHER BROTHERS OF ACORN FIELD HEIGHTS

Pumpkin Kisses & Harvest Wishes
Cinnamon Kisses & Forever Wishes
Secret Kisses & Twilight Wishes

Chapter One

SAWYER

Five-year-olds have zero respect for carefully laid plans. One second, Maple, my daughter, was holding my hand as we walked past Sugar & Spice Bakery—the establishment I'd been avoiding for two solid months —and the next, she yanked free and bolted straight for the green-awninged storefront like it was made of candy and wishes and unicorn sparkles.

"Maple!" The word came out strangled. I lunged after her, but she had the advantage of small size and complete lack of self-preservation instincts as she ran across the street. Thank goodness for small towns with little traffic. The bakery door swung open, the bell chiming with cheerful obliviousness, and my daughter disappeared inside.

I stood on the sidewalk for half a second, weighing my options. Let her go in alone and potentially get kidnapped by a pastry chef? Follow her and face the woman whose heart I broke seven years ago? Both options were terrible. But only one involved potential kidnapping, so I pushed through the door and immediately regretted the choice right away.

The bakery smelled like cinnamon and fresh bread, warm and sweet and so painfully familiar my chest tightened. I'd forgotten this smell, or maybe I'd tried to forget it. Isla always talked about opening a bakery that smelled like happiness, back when we were seventeen and stupid enough to make plans. Turned out she'd done it without me.

The interior was bigger than it looked from the outside. Display cases lined the left wall, full of pastries shaped like pumpkins and ghosts and things that probably tasted like heaven. Small tables with mismatched chairs filled the right side, each one decorated with a mason jar holding orange mums. Everything was exactly the kind of place Isla would create. Warm and welcoming and just different enough to be interesting.

And there, behind the counter, pulling a tray of something golden from the oven, was Isla Mercado herself.

Two months. I'd managed two months of careful route-planning and strange timing to avoid this exact moment. Two months of taking the long way around town, of grocery shopping at odd hours, of becoming the person who checked parking lots before getting out of his truck. All of it, wasted because my daughter really wanted a cookie.

Isla hadn't noticed us yet. She hummed under her breath while she worked, some song I didn't recognize, her blonde braid swinging as she moved. She wore a white apron covered in flour handprints and had a smudge of what looked like chocolate on her cheek. Seven years, and she still did that thing where she got completely absorbed in what she was doing, the rest of the world fading away.

Some things you don't forget, no matter how hard you try.

"Are you the cookie princess?" Maple's voice rang out across the bakery, loud and delighted and completely oblivious to the fact that she'd just destroyed my life. "Because this place smells like magic, and only princesses make magic cookies!"

Isla turned around. Her gaze landed on Maple first, and her expression softened into something warm and genuine and completely unguarded.

Then she looked up and saw me standing in the doorway like a coward, and every bit of warmth drained from her face.

For three seconds, nobody moved. The oven timer beeped. Somewhere in the back room, someone was hammering something. Outside, a car honked. But inside the bakery, time did this weird stuttering thing where I could see every expression that crossed Isla's face—surprise, recognition, hurt, anger, and then finally, nothing. Her features went blank, smooth like a mask sliding into place.

"Sawyer." She said my name like it was a diagnosis. Like she was confirming something unfortunate but entirely expected.

My throat was too dry. I swallowed twice before managing, "Hi."

Brilliant. Seven years of imagined conversations, and the best I could manage was "hi." My seventeen-year-old self would be ashamed. My current self was too busy trying not to bolt back out the door.

Maple tugged on my hand, bouncing on her toes. "Daddy, look, the cookie princess is real! Doesn't she look like a princess?"

Isla's gaze dropped back to Maple, and something shifted in her expression. She wiped her hands on her apron and moved toward the display case. "Cookie princess is a new one. Most people just call me Isla." She glanced at Maple, then back at me, and I watched her do the math. Five-year-old kid. My kid, obviously. Which meant—

Her jaw tightened. There it was. The moment she put together that I'd moved on, had a whole life after I left, while she was here building her bakery alone.

Except that wasn't the entire story, and I couldn't exactly explain it in front of Maple, so I stood there like an idiot while my daughter charmed the one person in town who had every reason to hate me.

"I'm Maple, and I'm almost six, and I really, really love your bakery." Maple pressed her face against the display case glass, leaving a small nose print. "It smells happy."

The corner of Isla's mouth twitched. Not quite a smile, but close enough that something in my chest did a painful flip. "It does, doesn't it?" She pulled out a pumpkin cookie decorated with a jack-o'-lantern face and placed it on a small plate. "That's the cinnamon. It's a happiness spice."

She handed the plate to Maple, and for a second our fingers almost touched as I reached out reflexively to help. We both jerked back as if we'd been burned.

Maple didn't notice. She was already cradling her cookie like it were made of gold, examining the jack-o'-lantern face. "This is the most beautiful cookie in the whole entire world. Can I eat it, or should we frame it?"

"You can eat it," Isla said. Her voice had that warm, patient tone she always used to use when explaining things, back when we were kids ourselves. "That's what cookies are for."

"My daddy said we couldn't come in here."

"I'm sure he did." Isla's gaze flicked to me. "Welcome back to town, by the way, Sawyer. I'd say it's good to see you, but we both know I'd be lying."

I deserved the bitterness in her tone. I deserved worse.

"How much for the cookie?"

Isla opened her mouth, but paused when Maggie did a little happy dance. A small smile broke across Isla's lips, and she sighed. "Don't worry about it."

"Really, I don't mind paying, and—"

From the back room, the hammering stopped. My youngest brother's voice called out, "Isla, where'd you want these shelves? The measurements aren't—" Asher appeared in the doorway, saw me, and stopped dead. "Oh. Sawyer. You're... here."

"And you're here. We were just leaving," I said, at the same time Maple said, "Can I sit at that table? Please? I don't want to drop crumbs on the floor because that would be rude, and Daddy says we're always polite to princesses."

Isla and I both opened our mouths. She got there first. "You can sit wherever you want."

Maple made a beeline for the table nearest the window, the one with the clearest view of the street and the pumpkin-shaped salt and pepper shakers. She settled into the chair, swinging her legs, and took the tiniest, most delicate bite of her cookie. Her eyes went wide.

"Daddy, this is the best cookie I've ever had. I'm going to marry this cookie."

"Pretty sure that's not legal, jellybean."

"Then you have to marry to princess who made it so I can have cookies all day." She looked at Isla with absolute seriousness. "Will you marry my daddy? He's very responsible. He makes my bed almost every day."

Isla's eyes went wide. "Oh, that's... wow. I think the better option is for you to come here when you need a little sugar."

4

I pulled out the chair across from Maple and sat, because standing in the middle of the bakery while my daughter proposed I marry my ex-girlfriend was far too awkward.

"Yikes..." Asher cleared his throat. "I should get back to—yeah." He disappeared into the back room without finishing the sentence, which was the smartest choice anyone had made all morning.

Isla turned back to her work, dismissing us. She moved around the kitchen area, pulling trays, checking temperatures, doing all the things that didn't require acknowledging my existence. I watched the stiffness of her shoulders, the way her hands moved a little too precisely, like she was concentrating very hard on not looking at me.

Maple took another microscopic bite of her cookie. "Do you make cookies every day?"

"Most days." Isla's voice was softer when she talked to Maple. Gentler. "Except Mondays. The bakery's closed on Mondays."

"What do you do on Mondays?"

"Sleep. Experiment with new recipes. Pretend I'm going to organize my apartment and then take a nap instead."

"Daddy's bad at organizing too. Our entire house is full of boxes. I wanna make a fort with them."

Isla's shoulders tensed. "Boxes?"

"Yeah. All our things are in them, which is why I can't make a fort yet, but—"

"Did you move back?" She directed the question to me, and I ran a hand through my hair and nodded.

"I'm surprised Dolores didn't tell you. That woman knows everything."

"How long ago?"

"Two months!" Maple's legs swung faster as she spoke. "We were staying at the farm with Uncle Levi, and there were chickens and goats and horses and cows and dogs and barn cats. The barn cats can't come inside. That's what Uncle Levi said. But we aren't living there anymore. We have a small house now. The boxes fill up the living room and I had, I had a dream that they tipped over and there was a big pile of stuff. Daddy's stuff and my stuff. And I went swimming in it. I'm starting kindergarten today, but then I ran away to come here because this bakery is the prettiest thing I've ever seen, and Daddy kept saying we'd come later, but later never comes, so I decided to make it now."

"Maple, eat your cookie," I murmured, nodding towards the cookie she'd nibbled like a mouse. When I glanced at Isla, she was standing with her hands on her hips, glaring at me. I rubbed the back of my neck. "Like she said, we've been back two months. Stayed with my brother until I got a lease. And we were supposed to be going to school, but Maple escaped from school drop-off. I'm still not sure how she did it. I looked away for half a second—"

"I'm sneaky," Maple announced proudly.

"You're grounded."

"What's grounded?"

"It's when you can't have dessert for a week."

Her face fell. "Oh. That's terrible. Can I be ungrounded if I finish all my vegetables?"

"We'll negotiate."

Isla had turned and stood with her back to us, hands braced on the counter, and tension ran up her spine. When she finally looked at me, her expression was carefully neutral again, but her eyes were bright in a way that made my stomach clench.

"Well, I'm sure you've been busy." She nodded at Maple's cookie. "Enjoy sweetheart. And like I said, welcome back to town, Sawyer. I'm sure we'll run into each other again, since it's a small town and all. I'll do my best to make it less painful for both of us."

The dismissal was clear. I should leave. Take Maple, get back to the truck, drive away and go back to my planned avoidance. But Maple was only halfway through her cookie, and she was finally, finally back to her happy self after two months of upheaval and custody threats and sleeping in unfamiliar places.

So I sat there while she ate, making appropriate noises at appropriate times while she chattered about cookie flavors and whether ghosts liked pumpkin spice. I tried not to watch Isla moving around her kitchen. Tried not to notice the way she still hummed under her breath when she worked. Tried not to think about the last time I'd seen her.

Tried and failed at all of it.

Maple finally finished, licking icing off her fingers. "Can we come back tomorrow?"

"We'll see."

"That means no." She sighed. "Grown-ups always say 'we'll see' when they mean no, but they think kids don't know that. We know that."

Before I could respond, my phone buzzed in my pocket. I pulled it out, glanced at the screen, and felt my stomach drop straight through the floor.

Unknown number. It was always bad news from unknown numbers these days.

The text was short.

> Mediation scheduled for October 21st, 9 AM. Bring proof of stable income and suitable childcare arrangements. Failure to appear will result in emergency custody evaluation.

I read it twice, trying to make the words say something different. They didn't.

Three weeks. I had three weeks to prove I deserved to keep my daughter. Three weeks to find a job that didn't involve mucking out stalls. Three weeks to establish childcare with people I barely knew anymore. Three weeks to convince a mediator that I was capable of being a single parent when I could barely manage to braid my daughter's hair without YouTube tutorials.

I looked up and found Isla watching me. Our eyes met and held for the first time since I'd walked through her door, and I watched her expression shift as she read whatever was on my face. The hardness softened, just barely, replaced by something that might have been concern if she weren't so determined to hate me.

"You okay?" The question came out reluctantly, like she'd tried to hold it back and failed.

"Yeah. Fine. Look, jellybean, we need to go. Come on."

Maple slid off her chair and made an elaborate curtsy toward Isla.

"Thank you for the magic cookie, Princess Isla. You're my new favorite person."

Isla curtsied back. "You're welcome, Princess Maple. You're my new favorite customer."

"Even better than the old ones?"

"Way better."

Maple beamed. She grabbed my hand and tugged me toward the door, chattering about how kindergarten was definitely going to be great now that she'd had a magic cookie for breakfast. I followed, letting her pull me along, and tried not to look back at Isla standing behind her counter with flour on her apron and questions in her eyes.

I failed at that too.

Outside, the October air was cool enough to make me wish I'd grabbed a jacket. The smell of wood smoke drifted from somewhere down the street, mixing with the scent of fallen leaves and distant rain. Main Street looked like a postcard of small-town autumn; pumpkins on stoops, scarecrows on benches, bunting in orange and black strung between lampposts. Picture perfect if you ignored the fact that my entire life was falling apart.

"Can we really come back?" Maple asked as I helped her into her booster seat.

"Maybe."

"That means no again, doesn't it?"

I buckled her in and pressed a kiss to the top of her head. Her hair smelled like the strawberry shampoo we'd used this morning, back when the worst thing I had to worry about was getting the braid straight. "That means I don't know yet. Let's get you to school before they send out a search party."

I closed her door, walked around to the driver's side, and let myself look back at the bakery one more time. Through the window, I could see Isla standing exactly where we'd left her, watching us. When she saw me looking, she turned away.

The story of us, really. One of us always turning away when the other one looked.

I started the truck—first try this time, small mercies—and pulled back onto Main Street. In the rearview mirror, Maple was already humming to herself, swinging her legs, completely unaware that she'd just torpedoed every plan I'd made since coming back to Acorn Field Heights.

My phone sat in the cup holder, the mediation text still glowing on the screen. October 21st.

The bakery disappeared behind us as I turned onto Oak Street. In three hours, I'd be back here to pick Maple up from her first day of kindergarten. In three weeks, I'd be sitting in the town hall with a mediator, fighting for the right to keep being her father.

Maybe I should've eaten a cookie too.

Chapter Two

ISLA

The Monday morning rush started at six and didn't stop. I burned two batches of cinnamon rolls before I admitted my hands wouldn't stop shaking. The third batch came out perfect, but by then I was forty-five minutes behind on a custom order, and Mrs. Norris was waiting at the counter with that expression that meant she'd already been standing there too long.

"I'm so sorry." I wiped flour from my forehead with the back of my wrist, leaving what probably looked like war paint. "Your apple turnovers are almost ready."

"Almost ready means not ready." Mrs. Norris tapped her watch. "I have a meeting at seven-thirty."

"Five minutes. I promise."

She didn't look convinced, but she stayed, which was more than I deserved given that her order should have been boxed and waiting when she arrived. I ducked back into the kitchen, where three custom orders sat in various states of completion, the pumpkin chocolate chip cookies only half-iced, and my prep work for tomorrow nowhere near done.

I was already drowning. Summer had been slow enough that I'd had to let Sadie go, my part-time helper who'd been with me since I opened.

Now October was here, and I was trying to do the work of two people while pretending everything was fine.

I pulled Mrs. Norris's turnovers from the oven, boxed them with fingers that fumbled the tissue paper twice, and brought them to the counter.

"Thank you for your patience."

She took the box, left exact change, and walked out without another word. The bell over the door chimed her exit, and I slumped against the counter.

The bakery smelled like burnt sugar and cinnamon, which was almost right except for the burnt part. Pumpkin-shaped cookies cooled on racks, waiting to be iced. A different order stared at me from the workspace. My feet already hurt, and it wasn't even seven.

This was fine. I was fine. I just needed to focus and stop thinking about hazel eyes and little girls in tutus and conversations that had turned my entire understanding of my past inside out.

The bell chimed again.

I looked up, forcing a smile, and the smile died on my face.

Sawyer stood in the doorway holding a crate of apples. Behind him, Maple clutched a smaller basket of what looked like tiny pumpkins, her purple tutu somehow even more elaborate than yesterday. A matching purple bow sat slightly crooked in her dark hair.

"We brought you things!" Maple announced, lugging her basket to the counter with both hands. "Daddy says you use apples for baking, and Uncle Levi had extras, so we brought them. And I picked out the baby pumpkins myself because they're the cutest."

Sawyer set his crate down near the door, his movements careful. He wasn't meeting my eyes. "We can leave them and go. I know you're busy. I just thought—Levi was going to drop them at the food bank anyway, and they're Honeycrisps, so I figured—" He stopped himself. "We'll get out of your way."

He remembered I liked Honeycrisps. After seven years, he remembered my preferred baking apple.

"Thank you." The words came out quieter than I meant them to. "That's—actually perfect timing. I have an order that needs apple filling."

Maple beamed. "See, Daddy? I told you she'd need them! I'm phys-kick." She stumbled over the word.

"Psychic," Sawyer corrected gently.

"That's what I said."

I moved toward the crate, intending to carry it to the back, but Sawyer was already lifting it. "Where do you want these?"

"You don't have to—"

"I know. But I'm here, and they're heavy, so just tell me where. Jelly-bean, stay out here."

"But I wanna see the kitchen."

I pointed towards a corner I'd dressed up for some of the other kids in town. It was the most decorated part of the bakery, and I'd printed out free Halloween coloring pages and bought a box of crayons for them to use. "There are some pumpkins there that need to be colored. Can you help me Princess Maple?"

She flashed a bright smile at me and bobbed her head. "Okay!"

Sawyer mouthed "thank you" to me. I shrugged and led him through to the kitchen, acutely aware of him behind me, of how small the space felt with both of us in it. The kitchen that had felt like mine— my sanctuary, my safe place—now held the boy I'd spent most of my adult life trying to forget.

Except he wasn't a boy anymore. The arms carrying that crate were solid with work. His frame had filled out beneath his red flannel. A few grey hairs were showing in his dark hair, which I had a feeling had to do with the five-year-old princess following him around.

"Counter's fine." My voice came out steadier than I felt.

He set the crate down, and I saw him take in the chaos; the half-finished orders, the cooling racks covering every surface, the dishes piled in the sink. His brow furrowed, but he didn't comment. Just stood there looking like he wanted to say something and couldn't figure out how.

"You're behind," he said finally.

"I'm fine, thank you very much," I snapped.

"That's not what I—" He stopped. Tried again. "You're doing the work of two people."

"Three, actually, if you count the business management and the social media and the ordering." I pulled out a knife and started peeling apples. "But it's fine. I've got it under control."

"Isla—"

"I said I'm fine."

We stood there in silence, broken only by the sound of my knife against apple skin. Too fast, too aggressive, my mother would have said. Like I was fighting the fruit instead of preparing it.

"You're tempering that too hot."

I looked up. Sawyer was pointing at the double boiler on the stove, where I'd started melting chocolate.

"I know what I'm doing."

"I'm sure you do. But it's at 129 degrees right now, and most chocolate seizes above 130." He moved closer, not touching me but close enough that I could smell soap and autumn air. "Lower heat, constant stirring. Learned that from a YouTube video when Maple wanted fancy hot chocolate."

I stared at him. "You learned chocolate tempering from YouTube."

"I learned a lot of things from YouTube. I think it's taught me more than school ever did." He rubbed the back of his neck. "Turns out single dads who can't afford takeout get creative. Started with mac and cheese, moved up to actual meals. Then Maple discovered baking shows, and she wanted to try everything, so I had to figure out how not to poison us both with undercooked cookies."

"You bake."

"Badly. Mostly. But I'm getting better." His mouth curved. "Last week I made bread that was only partially hockey-puck consistency."

Despite everything—despite the chaos and the exhaustion and the fact that my anger was crumbling—my lips twitched. "Impressive."

"I'm a man of many mediocre talents."

I turned back to the apples, but I lowered the heat on the double boiler. Because he was right, and I knew it, and pretending otherwise would just mean ruining an order.

Sawyer picked up a second knife and started peeling apples without asking.

"You don't have to help."

"I know." He focused on his apple. "But Maple's going to be

coloring in your kids' corner for at least twenty minutes, and you're drowning, and I'm here, so I might as well make myself useful."

"I'm not drowning."

"I smell burnt sugar."

I went still. "It's a bakery. Sometimes things burn and—"

"You've got that line between your eyebrows that means you're stressed, and there's flour in your hair, and your apron's on inside out."

I looked down. My apron was definitely inside out.

"Also," he continued, still peeling, "you mixed up Mrs. Norris's order. She comes in every Monday for apple turnovers, and you gave her the cherry ones by mistake last week. Maple mentioned it to me because Mrs. Norris mentioned it to the entire post office, apparently."

Heat flooded my face. I'd been so proud of catching that mistake before Mrs. Norris left. Except apparently she'd noticed anyway and just been too polite—or too judgmental—to say anything.

"I'm getting a new assistant soon." Not exactly true. I didn't have the time to look for one. "Just taking some time to find the right person."

"Sure." Sawyer finished his apple, reached for another. "Because there are so many trained bakers in Acorn Field Heights just waiting to work part-time for whatever you can afford to pay them."

"You don't know what I can afford."

"I know what struggling looks like." His voice went quiet. "I've been doing it for five years."

The kitchen felt smaller. I focused on my apple, on the spiral of skin coming away from flesh, on anything except the fact that Sawyer was standing in my back kitchen helping me as if he hadn't left in the first place.

"Why are you doing this?" The question escaped before I could stop it. "Helping me. Being nice. Acting like—" I stopped myself.

"Acting like what?"

"Like we're friends. Like any of this is normal."

He set down his knife. "I'm doing this because my daughter thinks you're magic, and I'm trying to be the kind of dad who doesn't mess up every good thing that comes into her life." His throat worked. "And because even if you hate me, which you should, I can't walk into your bakery and watch you struggle without at least offering to help. Even if that makes me pathetic."

"It doesn't make you pathetic."

"No? What does it make me?"

I looked at him then. At the exhaustion in his eyes and the careful way he held himself and the fact that he was here, in my kitchen, peeling apples because his daughter was coloring in my kids' corner and I was drowning and he noticed.

"Kind," I said finally. "It makes you kind."

He picked up his knife again, and we worked in silence that felt less sharp than before.

We finished the apples in twenty minutes, working side by side in a rhythm that shouldn't have felt so natural. Sawyer measured spices while I rolled dough, and when I reached for the cinnamon, he handed it to me before I could ask. Like muscle memory. Like we'd done this before, even though we never had. He wasn't here when I started my bakery. He'd already left.

"Miss Isla!" Maple's voice rang from the front. "I finished coloring the pumpkins! Can I do the ghosts now?"

"All of them?" I moved to the doorway, wiping my hands on my apron. Every single coloring page was filled in, pumpkins and cats and witches colored. "That's impressive."

"I'm very good at staying in the lines." She held up a ghost page. "Daddy says it's my superpower."

"Everyone needs a superpower." I glanced at Sawyer, who was washing his hands at the sink. "Your dad's is apparently YouTube baking tutorials."

Maple giggled. "He watches them on his phone when he thinks I'm sleeping. Last week he made cookies that were flat like pancakes, and we had to eat them with a spoon."

"They were practice cookies," Sawyer defended.

"They were soup cookies." Maple grinned at him with so much love it made my chest ache. "But I ate them anyway because Daddy tried really hard."

She really loved him—the way she looked at him like he was safety and home, the way he looked at her like she was the only thing in the world that mattered. It complicated my anger toward him.

"We should go." Sawyer dried his hands. "You've got work to do, and we've taken up enough of your morning."

"But I didn't get to see the magic kitchen!" Maple's face fell. "I want to see where the cupcakes are made."

"Maple—"

"It's fine." The words came out before I could think them through. "She can see the kitchen for five minutes. But she has to stay out of the way, and she can't touch anything hot."

Maple's eyes went wide. "Really? I can see where the magic happens?"

"There's no magic. Just butter and sugar and a lot of dirty dishes."

"That's what magic is," Maple said solemnly. "Making something from nothing. Like princesses. Or cookies."

I couldn't help it. I smiled.

The kitchen tour lasted longer than five minutes. Maple wanted to know about every piece of equipment, every ingredient, why some spices came in jars and some in bags, whether the standing mixer had a name, and if cookies really did taste better with love added to the recipe.

"They do," I told her, showing her the vanilla beans I used for special orders. "But love is expensive, so mostly I use good butter and real vanilla."

"Daddy says love is free."

"Your daddy's very wise."

Sawyer, leaning against the doorframe with his arms crossed, made a sound that might have been a laugh. "First time anyone's called me wise in about seven years."

Seven years. The number we kept circling around without saying what it meant.

Maple, oblivious, moved to the cooling racks. "Can I help make cookies? Daddy lets me pour things and crack eggs, and I'm very careful not to get shells in the bowl."

"That's an important skill." I glanced at Sawyer. "Does she really?"

"She's actually better at it than I am." Pride colored his voice. "Gentle hands. Better coordination than her old man."

"I get it from Mommy." Maple said it matter-of-factly, without the weight the word should have carried. "She was good at pretty things. Daddy's good at fixing things. I'm good at both."

The casual mention of her mother made Sawyer's shoulders tense. I watched him fight whatever he wanted to say, watched him choose silence instead.

"You know what?" I heard myself say. "I do have a kids' baking class on Saturdays. Starting this weekend. If you want to learn properly, you'd be welcome."

Maple's face lit up like I'd just offered her the moon. "Really? I can learn to make magic cupcakes like the Boo-Berry ones?"

"Really."

"Did you hear that, Daddy?" She grabbed his hand. "I'm going to be a real baker! Just like Miss Isla! This is the best thing that's ever happened!"

Sawyer looked at me with an expression that was part gratitude, part confusion, and part something I didn't want to name. "You're sure? I can pay for the class—"

"Oh, I expect you to pay. It's fifty dollars for the two hour session. Covers ingredients and the mess." I crossed my arms. "Every town needs trained bakers."

"Thank you." The words came out rough. "This means—you have no idea what this means."

I did, though. I could see it in the way Maple was already planning her future as a baker, in the way Sawyer looked at his daughter like she was the best thing he'd ever done.

The bell over the front door chimed. Voices drifted back— customers arriving, people who needed coffee and pastries and small talk about the weather.

"I should get back to work." I moved toward the door, away from Sawyer and his complicated eyes. Nodding towards the front of the store, I led them out of the kitchen. Maple bounded over to the kids corner and picked up a few of the coloring sheets she'd filled in. I'd have to print more out soon, whenever I had a spare moment. "See you Saturday, Maple. Nine o'clock. Don't be late."

"I won't! I'm never late! Daddy says being on time is a superpower too!" She hugged her coloring pages to her chest. "Thank you, Miss Isla."

"You're very welcome."

They left, Sawyer with one hand on Maple's shoulder, guiding her across the street. I watched them go, my hands clenched in my inside out apron.

Then I turned back to my chaos. Multiple unfinished cookies, the pile of dirty dishes, three custom orders that still needed finishing. The work of running a bakery alone when the bakery had grown beyond what one person could manage.

I lasted forty minutes before I had to admit defeat. My mind and my body were exhausted, and I glanced at the apples Sawyer had brought. Perfectly chosen, exactly what I needed. He'd remembered. After seven years of silence, he'd remembered that I preferred Honeycrisps for baking because they held their texture and had the right balance of tart and sweet.

"Okay, Jane," I whispered to my sourdough starter, bubbling quietly on the counter. "Here's where we are. The boy I used to love came back with a daughter. He remembers my preferred apples. He notices when I'm drowning. And I just agreed to teach his daughter to bake because I'm either very forgiving or very stupid."

Jane bubbled. No judgment. No answers.

I pressed my palms against the counter. "And I don't know what to do with that. I don't know how to be angry at someone who's been gone for two years and clearly had an entire life started without me in it. I don't know how to forgive Sawyer. I don't know—"

The bell chimed again. More customers. New orders. All the while pretending to have everything under control.

I straightened my apron—fixed it right-side-out this time—and went back to work. Because that's what I did when the world shifted under my feet. I kept going. I made the next batch of cookies. I tried again.

The bakery closed at six. By six-fifteen, I'd cleaned the front, started the dishwasher, and was working on the last of the custom orders when someone knocked on the locked door.

I looked up, ready to point at the "Closed" sign, and froze.

My mother stood on the other side of the glass, her silver-streaked blonde hair pulled back, her expression the one that meant she knew something I didn't want her to know.

I thought about pretending I hadn't seen her. Thought about turning off the lights and hiding in the kitchen until she left.

Instead, I unlocked the door.

"Mama."

"Isla." She swept in, bringing the smell of her perfume and the cool evening air. "I heard you had visitors this morning."

"Dolores told you?"

"Dolores told me." She settled at the counter like she owned it, which in a way she did—she'd cosigned the loan that let me open this place. "Sawyer Thatcher and his daughter. Brought you apples."

"They did."

"And you invited the little one to your baking class."

"I did."

My mother studied me with eyes that saw too much. "You're being careful, I hope."

"Careful of what?"

"Of boys who left you once already. Of building hope on foundations that crumbled before."

The words I'd been holding back finally broke free. "Did you know?"

She went very still. "Know what?"

"That Sawyer was back." My voice shook. "Did you know?"

She didn't respond right away, biting her thumbnail.

"You knew."

"I did." She reached across the counter for me. "Your father and I wanted to protect you from having your heart broken again. You know we only have your best interests in mind."

"Yeah, sure. But it's a small town, Mama. I was bound to find out at some point."

"We were hoping he'd leave again before that day. Unfortunately, that didn't work out. We've seen the Thatcher boys over the years— always struggling, always barely getting by after their father's heart attack. We just want you to be careful. Wouldn't want you to be hurt again."

I stiffened, pulling my hand away. "I was hurt back then, but I'm an adult and I can make my own decisions."

"What are you going to do?"

"I don't know."

"And Sawyer?"

"I don't know that either." I turned back to the work that needed finishing. "But I'll figure it out."

"Just be careful. That boy is trouble."

"Maybe the boy was, but this man is different. He's a father now. He's... He's changed. And so did I." I wiped down the counter again even though I'd done it ten minutes earlier. It was just something to do with my hands while I verbally processed. "Anyway, I've got to get started on tomorrow's prep, Mama. I'll see you later."

My mother left after extracting a promise that I'd come to dinner in the next few weeks. I locked the door behind her and stood in my empty bakery, surrounded by the evidence of a day spent drowning and being rescued by the last person I'd expected.

Once everything was cleaned, prepped, and reorganized, I printed out a couple more coloring pages and stacked them on the table in the corner. The extra pages Maple had colored were strewn across the surface, and I considered throwing them away. Instead, I grabbed a roll of tape and put a few of them up on the corner walls. They were festive. That was all.

That finished, I picked up my phone and pulled up the website for the local job boards. My fingers hovered over the "Post a Job" button. I sighed, and set the phone down.

Because the truth was, I couldn't afford to hire anyone. Not really. Not unless business picked up substantially. October was good but not that good. I was barely covering my costs most months, living off thin margins and the hope that next year would be better.

But I also couldn't keep doing this alone. Couldn't keep burning batches and missing orders and pretending everything was fine when I was one bad day away from losing everything I'd built.

I needed help. Maybe I could get Sadie to come back if I pleaded. At least I knew her, which would be better than having to go through a list of strangers applying online. But typing up the job request information would take time and brain capacity, and I decided that would have to be a future Isla problem because what I needed most was a nap. A really, really long nap.

Chapter Three

SAWYER

I forgot how judgmental the Acorn Valley Heights church pews could be. Not the actual pews—they were just wood and eighty years of hymnal damage. But the people sitting in them had apparently spent the past six weeks speculating about Sawyer Thatcher's return, and now they had a chance to stare without pretending they weren't staring. Thankfully, I was also sharing the heat with my older brother's old fling, who'd also returned recently. Now it wasn't just gossip about me, and the daughter I'd shown up with. Amberlyn Avery's name also floated around the room where there should've just been prayers and confessions.

There were too many whispered conversations behind bulletins. Mrs. Patterson from the post office turned completely around in her pew, her enormous hat wobbling with the effort. Mayor Goldwin watched from three rows away.

Maple swung her legs next to me, oblivious in her purple tutu and Sunday cardigan. "Why's everyone looking at us?"

"They're not."

"That lady with the giant hat just did it again."

I glanced over. Mrs. Patterson whipped back around so fast her neck made a sound like cracking branches. Behind her, Dolores didn't even bother hiding her interest, notebook open on her lap like she was documenting evidence.

"Maybe they're admiring your tutu," I whispered.

"Obviously. It's very pretty." Maple smoothed the purple fabric. "But I think they're mostly looking at you, Daddy. You're very tall."

I pulled her closer, and she leaned into my side, still swinging those light-up sneakers that blinked pink with every bump.

A row ahead of me, my older brother, Levi, sat with the woman he'd hired to examine our soil compositions. Dr. Li, I think he said her name was. I hadn't really paid attention when he'd introduced us. My job was to help on the farm. Not run it. Any soil problems were Levi problems. And by the way Levi kept turning his head to look at Amberlyn Avery, who was with her family near the front, he had more than just soil composition to think about. I was going to poke him in the back and tease him, as was my duty as the middle brother, but that's when I saw her.

Isla sat four rows away on the opposite side, long braid down her back, green dress that made me think thoughts that had no place in church. Next to her sat a man with silver hair and ramrod posture. Her father. The man who'd handed me twenty thousand dollars and a collection of very logical reasons why I wasn't good enough for his daughter. I wondered if Isla knew about that. If she'd ever learned that her father had offered to pay me to leave her.

My jaw locked. Maple felt me tense, looked up with worried eyes that were far too perceptive. I forced myself to relax, or at least fake it well enough to fool a five-year-old.

The service crawled by. People stood, started the shuffle toward coffee hour in the fellowship hall. Maple grabbed my hand and pulled me into the aisle.

Right into Isla's path.

We stopped. The crowd flowed around us while what felt like the entire congregation watched to see what would happen next.

"Hi," I managed.

"Hi."

Maple had zero sense of awkward social dynamics. I envied her most days. "Miss Isla! You're here! Do you come here every Sunday? Will you sit with us next time?"

"Maple—"

"Isla." Her father appeared at her elbow. "Mr. Thatcher. I see you've been busy the last seven years," he said, raising an eyebrow as he glanced down at my daughter. I clenched my hand into a fist behind my back and opened my mouth to respond, but he spoke instead. "Isla, we need to leave."

"Coffee hour, Dad. I told Mom I'd help serve." She glanced at her father, then at me, then at Maple's hopeful expression. "I'm staying. You can tell Mom I'll get a ride."

"But—"

"I'll see you later, Dad." She stepped out from under his hand.

He clenched his jaw, sent a glare at me, and then left, his footsteps echoing off tile.

"Was that your daddy?" Maple asked, a frown on her face.

Isla crouched down to Maple's level. "You're very observant, aren't you? Yes, that's my daddy."

"I don't think your daddy likes my daddy."

I snorted and quickly covered it by rubbing my mouth. "Maple, go find Uncle Asher for me, and remind him that he promised to come help set up your bed in your new room."

"Okay," she ran off without hesitation, and Isla stood up.

"I'm sorry about my dad. I'm sure he likes you, he's just—"

"It's fine, Isla. Like you said, my daughter's observant. She notices things a lot of people miss." I shoved my hands into my pockets. "I've got to go talk to Ash, but it was good to see you. Thanks for teaching Maple yesterday, by the way. She wouldn't stop talking about how much she enjoyed your baking class."

Isla looked like she wasn't ready to change topics, but she sighed and nodded. "She knows a lot for a five-year-old. If she wanted to be a baker, I bet she'd do well. She's a smart girl."

I smiled, raising on my tiptoes and leaning to keep my daughter in sight as she wove through the room towards my younger brother. "She is. I'm proud to be her dad. Look, I see Ash, so I'll talk to you later, yeah?"

"Oh, yeah. I guess. Bye," she said, giving an awkward wave as I nodded once and headed the direction Maple had gone.

In all honesty, I didn't really need to speak to Asher about putting together Maple's bed. I could do it myself. But it was a good excuse to leave the conversation before my impulsiveness ruined Isla's perception of her father by telling her about the bribe he'd offered all those years ago.

I certainly wasn't father of the year, but I doubted Mr. Mercado was either.

On Monday morning, I was ankle-deep in horse manure when my phone buzzed in my pocket. Levi's name popped up with a text, and I swore if it was a message telling me to do the pig pens next, I was going to chuck my phone into the pile I'd just made. He'd already sent me to the goat pen and the chicken coup. When I'd returned to the farm asking for a job, I'd obviously forgotten how much it literally stank.

Thankfully, it wasn't about shoveling more poop.

> Isla needs more apples for her Fall treats. Bring a crate down to the bakery when you get a chance. Maybe hose off first. I'm sure you smell...

I wiped my hands on my jeans and glanced at my watch. Maple was in kindergarten for a couple more hours, and the bakery wasn't too far into town. This could work. I took the worlds fastest shower and loaded a crate into the back of my truck while my hair was still dripping.

When I got to the bakery, the smell of cinnamon and sugar hit me before I even stepped inside, and I hesitated for a moment, wondering if I should've called ahead. But the bell jingled when I pushed the door open, and Isla looked up from the counter, her hands dusted with flour.

"Hey," she said, surprise flickering across her face. "Didn't expect to see you here so soon."

"Levi said you needed apples." I hefted the crate onto the counter, the weight digging into my arms.

"Oh, right, thanks." She wiped her hands on her apron and peeked inside the crate. "These look perfect. I'm doing an apple caramel tart this week, and I'm almost out."

"Apple caramel tart, huh? Sounds fancy."

She shrugged, but there was a spark of pride in her eyes. "It's my twist on a classic. People seem to like it."

I leaned against the counter, noting the way she avoided looking directly at me. Her braid was slung over one shoulder, and she had a streak of flour on her cheek. "So, what's it like? Running the bakery you've always wanted?"

She paused, her hands hovering over the crate. "You remember that?"

"Of course. You used to talk about it all the time. Even in elementary school. You'd draw pictures of it during class."

"Okay, first of all, that's embarrassing," she laughed, but her cheeks flushed pink. "But yeah, it's... it's everything I thought it would be. And also nothing like I thought it would be."

"How so?"

She motioned for me to follow her to the kitchen in the back, where trays of cookies were cooling on racks. "It's a lot of work. Long hours, early mornings, and a constant stream of 'what if this fails?' But then there are moments when everything just clicks, and it's worth it."

"Like teaching Maple how to frost cupcakes? She demanded we get icing bags so she could practice."

She smiled at that, her face softening. "Yeah, like that. She's a quick learner."

"She doesn't get that from me," I said without thinking, then winced. "I didn't mean—"

"It's fine," she blurted, turning back to the cookies. "How's she doing with kindergarten?"

"She loves it. Came home yesterday and told me she's going to be a baker when she grows up." I grinned. "Thanks to you."

Isla laughed. "I'm just encouraging her dreams. Here—" she handed me a piping bag filled with orange icing. "Help me decorate these pumpkin cookies. I bet you're a quick study too."

"I'm really not."

"Just try. I have extras, and you can't mess it up too badly."

"Famous last words," I muttered, but I took the bag anyway. She demonstrated the technique—outlining the edges first, letting it set, then filling in the middle—while I watched, trying to commit it to memory. My first attempt was... well, let's just say it looked more like a blob than a pumpkin.

"Not bad," she said with a chuckle.

"Liar." I laughed, shaking my head. "Maple's probably way better at this than I am."

"Practice," she said, bumping my shoulder with hers. "And maybe a little natural talent."

"Oh, definitely natural talent." I glanced at her, caught the way her eyes crinkled when she smiled, and quickly looked back at the cookies.

Somehow, I managed to get icing on my ear. And in my hair. And on the counter. Isla was laughing so hard she had to sit down, and I couldn't help but join in. "This is ridiculous," I said, swiping at the mess with a rag.

"Here," she said, still giggling, and before I knew it, she'd dabbed a bit of icing on my cheek.

My mouth dropped open. "Did you just—"

"I had to even it out. You already had some on the other side," she said, her eyes sparkling. But then her phone dinged on the counter, and the moment dissolved. She glanced at it quickly, then went back to her cookies.

My own phone went off, and I pulled it out still smiling, expecting a text from Levi or Asher. Instead, it was Jen. The smile dropped off my face immediately.

> Just wanted to remind you about the mediation on the 21st. I'm sure Maple's been asking about me. Maybe we could arrange a visit before then?

My stomach dropped. I'd been avoiding thinking about the mediation. I hadn't even started looking for another job yet.

"Everything okay?" Isla asked.

"Yeah, it's just... my ex. Maple's mom." I hesitated, then figured I might as well be honest. "She's threatening to take Maple. Has been for a while. She... She thinks I'm not a stable enough parent. We've got a mediation in a couple weeks to try and work it out. If we can't, she'll take full custody."

Isla set down the piping bag and turned to face me fully. "Sawyer..."

"It's fine," I said quickly, even though it wasn't. "I'm figuring it out."

"You're a good dad," she said, her voice firm. "From what little I've seen, you're doing everything right."

I didn't know what to say to that, so I just nodded, the weight of her kindness and my own inadequacy pressing down on me.

"Thanks," I muttered, glancing at the clock on the wall. "I should probably head out. Need to pick up Maple soon." I really didn't, but I also didn't want to stick around and dive into how my marriage failed and now it felt like my ex was out to take everything from me. She'd already gotten the house, the car, and half the money. But I'd give all of that ten times over as long as I got to keep my daughter.

"Right." She hesitated, like she wanted to say more, but then just nodded. "Thanks for helping with the cookies. And for the apples."

"Anytime." I grabbed my keys, feeling the icing in my hair as I ran my fingers through it. "Guess I'll be taking some of your decorating skills home with me," I said, pointing to the orange streaks in my dark hair.

She smiled, but it didn't quite reach her eyes. "Keep practicing. You'll get there."

I gave her a quick wave and hurried out the door, the bell jingling behind me. The truck felt too small, my thoughts too big, and I sat there for a minute, staring at the steering wheel.

Jen's text was still on my screen, and I couldn't shake the fear that no matter what I did, it wouldn't be enough. I didn't want to lose Maple. I couldn't.

Chapter Four

ISLA

"But Miss Isla, ghosts are sparkly," Maple insisted on Thursday afternoon, brandishing the glitter shaker like a weapon. "Everyone knows that."

"I'm not sure everyone knows that, princess."

"Well, they should." She dumped approximately half a container onto one cookie. It was instantly inedible. I chuckled as she beamed at me. "There. Now he's fancy."

Maple had arrived at my bakery after kindergarten. Third day in a row. Purple tutu somewhat worse for wear, light-up sneakers blinking with each bounce. The first day, I'd assumed it was a one-time thing, and Sawyer assured me it was. The second day, I'd realized it was becoming a pattern, and he apologized. Today, I'd accepted my fate and set up a decorating station at the corner table. I didn't complain, though, because, for the hour or so that she was here, so was her dad, and he was insistent that he help while Maple stayed busy in the corner.

And with six custom orders due in a day. Fall festival prep looming. And a potential win for the bakery at the baking contest during the festival, I needed help where I could get it. Even if help made most of my bats look more like black rotten bananas.

"Look what I made at school!" Maple spread a drawing across the table when I checked on her progress. Crayon figures with stick arms and wide smiles, surrounded by what might have been cookies or possibly abstract beach balls. "It's us making cookies together! See? That's you with the big spoon, me with the sprinkles, and Daddy trying not to mess up. He's getting better though!"

I studied the three figures. Stick people holding hands in front of an oven, surrounded by what looked like flying cookies. "This is beautiful."

"I know. My teacher said I'm very creative," She examined her work. "I drew us as a team! Like the Avengers but with cupcakes!"

The Avengers. Not a family. Not a couple. A team. I could work with that.

"We're like a superhero team," Maple continued, warming to her theme. "Daddy's the strong one, you're the smart one, and I'm the cute one."

"That's a good team." I handed her a piping bag filled with black icing. "Now give these ghosts some faces while I go check on the oven."

When I walked to the kitchen in the back, Sawyer was leaning over the stand mixer, frowning.

"Uh oh," I said walking up beside him. "I don't like that look."

"I can't remember if I added salt." He rubbed the heel of his wrist over his forehead.

A customer came in before I could respond, and I bit my lip. "I'll—"

"I'll go take care of that," he said, nodding towards the front. "Sorry!"

He didn't have to apologize. I much preferred the work in the back. Grabbing a clean spoon, I dipped it into the mixture and tried it. Nope. Definitely no salt. I grabbed a toddler's handful and dropped it into the giant bowl.

Sawyer came back as I finished mixing it. "Did I—"

"Yes. I fixed it. Who was that?"

"Art from the hardware store on his lunch break. Wanted a croissant." Sawyer leaned against the counter as I moved the giant bowl to the counter, dumping out the dough onto the floured surface. He kept talking as I rolled my sleeves up. "I left Maple at the table. She had icing on her nose and what appeared to be seventeen cookies in various states of ghost-dom arranged in front of her. One of them is apparently named Boobear."

"That seems appropriate," I said, chuckling.

"He's a gentleman ghost with a mustache. Oscar has the hat. He's fancy." He leaned forward with a smirk. "You know, in case she quizzes you later."

The bell chimed again. Another customer. Then another. The afternoons were usually slow, but apparently everyone in Acorn Field Heights had decided they needed baked goods today. By the time four-thirty rolled around, Sawyer had helped twelve customers while I'd burned my hand on a hot pan, finished two more batches of cookies, came up with an idea for my cake for the Fall Festival baking competition, and nearly chopped off a finger when opening a supply box.

Sawyer took one look at my face and said, "Everything okay?"

"I'm fine." I wiped my hands on my apron, leaving flour streaks. "How's Maple?"

"Covered in glitter, probably for eternity. I sent her to clean up in the bathroom." He examined the cookie army on the corner table. "Is that one wearing a crown?"

"That's Princess Ghost," Maple informed him as she came back, a paper towel scrunched in her little hands. "She rules the ghost kingdom."

"Obviously." His mouth curved, and I caught myself staring at the way his whole face changed when he smiled at his daughter. He swooped her up into his arms and kissed her on the cheek. "You're pretty talented there, kid." When he turned to me, the smile stayed, and I tried to remember to breathe. "Do you need help with anything else?"

"I—" The answer was yes. I appreciated his help, and yet I still felt years behind. "I'm okay."

They left with a box of Maple's creations and a promise to return tomorrow. After they'd gone, I stood in my empty bakery and realized I'd forgotten to eat lunch. Again. The custom orders still needed finishing. The fall festivities were starting up soon. And I had no idea how I was going to manage all of it.

Something had to change. I just didn't know what.

The night of the hayride, the air smelled like fallen leaves and hot cider. It was getting colder, and I shivered as I shoved my hands deeper into my jacket pockets. My booth was nestled between a caramel apple stand and a display of hand-knit scarves, the last of my pumpkin-spiced muffins already on display. Amberlyn Avery leaned against the folding table, her fingers wrapped tight around a paper cup.

"So what do you think?" she asked, sipping the cider.

"I like the idea." I twisted the end of my braid between my fingers. "Your family's honey in my pastries? That's smart business."

Her shoulders loosened. "I'm so glad! Do you have time to talk business this week?"

"I'm sure I can find time." I wasn't sure, but she didn't need to know that.

"What are you two talking about?" A familiar voice drawled.

"Business," Amberlyn responded without turning.

I turned just as Levi, Sawyer's older brother, stepped into the glow of the string lights overhead, arms crossed. He wasn't looking at me, though. His gaze was locked on Amberlyn. "Well, we got fifteen minutes before the next ride. You ready to go?"

Amberlyn sighed, tossing her empty cup into the recycling bin. "I suppose I could be ready."

Levi scratched the back of his neck. "How's the booth going, Isla? Has my brother been around?"

I tried to hide my flush. "I haven't seen Sawyer, no. But—"

A shriek cut through the chatter of the crowd.

"Isla!"

I barely had time to brace before Maple barreled into my legs, her tiny fists clutching the hem of my sweater. She was bundled in a puffy pink coat, a handmade felt crown slipping sideways over her curls.

"Hi," I laughed, crouching to her level. "You look very royal tonight."

She puffed her chest out. "I am royal. I'm the Queen of the Hayride!"

Behind her, Sawyer stopped just short of plowing into us, his hands raised in surrender, his cheeks pink from the cold. "She sprinted the second she saw you." He glanced at his brother, who had a wide smirk over his lips that he wasn't bothering to hide. Amberlyn offered a small smile too. "Hey Lee, Amberlyn."

"Hey yourself. Let's go," Levi said, guiding Amberlyn away. He tossed a wink over his shoulder to his brother that I tried not to overthink.

Maple drew my attention back to her, bouncing on her toes. "Can we go on the hayride now? With you? Please? Daddy said only if you say yes."

I glanced up at Sawyer, who lifted one shoulder in a sheepish shrug. "She's been planning this all day."

"I have a booth to run, and—"

"I'll take care of it, dear," Sawyer's Aunt Caroline said, coming over and patting Maple on the head. "You go have fun."

The next thing I knew, I was squeezed between a chattering five-year-old and Sawyer on a creaking hay bale; the tractor lurching forward beneath us. Maple immediately clambered onto my lap, her cold fingers twisting into my jacket.

"You're warm," she announced.

Sawyer chuckled under his breath. "You're basically using her as a space heater, kid."

"Yep." Maple snuggled closer. "And you're my back warmer."

The night air numbed my nose, my breath curling white in the dim light. Despite the crowd around us, it felt oddly private—just the three of us pressed together, the rumble of the tractor beneath us, Amberlyn's voice drifting over the speaker as she narrated the history of the valley.

Sawyer shifted beside me, his knee brushing mine.

"You cold?" His fingers skimmed my shoulder, just above where the jacket slipped off.

"A little."

Before I could blink, he unwound the thick plaid scarf from his own neck and looped it around mine. His knuckles grazed my jaw as he adjusted it.

"There."

His voice was low, quiet in a way that made me forget how to breathe.

Maple hummed happily, twisting to look at the passing landscape.

The rest of the ride passed in a blur of Maple's questions ("Do pumpkins grow all year?") and Sawyer's deep laughter when I made up elaborate answers. By the time Levi circled the tractor back around, my cheeks hurt from smiling.

Maple yawned, her head drooping against my collarbone as we stepped off the wagon. Sawyer caught my eye as she rubbed her fists into her sockets, nodding toward the parking lot.

"I'll walk you to your booth," he said.

The festival was still bustling, but the crowd had thinned, the lantern light golden against the night. Maple was half-asleep in Sawyer's arms by the time we reached my display. He adjusted his grip, bouncing her slightly before speaking.

"I, uh. I just wanted to say..." His throat worked, like he was forcing the words out. "What you're doing for Maple. Letting her hang out at the bakery so often. Letting her do baking classes. Indulging her tonight." He hesitated. "It means a lot."

"Don't thank me," I murmured, reaching out to tuck Maple's wild curls away from her face. "She's easy to love."

His fingers curled tighter around his daughter, but his gaze never left mine. "Yeah," he mumbled. "She really is. Look, I... I was wondering if you'd like more help. Maple's going to spend the day with my aunt tomorrow and I know you've got a lot going on and—"

"Yes," I said before he'd finished. "I absolutely need help."

"Oh. Good. I'll um... I'll be there tomorrow, then?"

"Tomorrow."

"Good."

"Great."

Then he turned and walked away, the night swallowing him up—but the ghost of his scarf stayed wrapped around me, still warm from his skin.

Chapter Five

SAWYER

I showed up at the bakery fifteen minutes early with three types of apples and two sizes of pumpkins. Through the window, Isla moved around the kitchen. She'd pinned printed recipe cards to a corkboard, organized ingredients in neat rows, and set up two workstations like we were filming a cooking show. Her hair was already escaping its bun, and even from here, tension filled her shoulders.

She looked up, saw me, and something flickered across her face before she came to unlock the door. Not quite a smile, but close.

"You're early," she said.

"Didn't want to give you time to reconsider." I held up the produce box. "Brought options. Honeycrisps, Granny Smiths, and Macouns. Also two pumpkin sizes in case we need variety."

"Look at you, being prepared." She stepped back to let me in, and the bakery's warmth hit me along with the smell of yeast and cinnamon. "I'm impressed."

"Fair warning though, my piping skills are still questionable."

"We'll work on it." She directed me to the prep station where she'd laid out measuring cups, mixing bowls, and enough spices to stock a small store. "So here's the plan. We'll start with the turnovers, then do the cakes, and finish with cookies."

"You've thought this through."

"You could say that." She pulled out a laminated timeline. "We'll start with how to roast pumpkin, then move to the dough and decorating."

"You're the boss."

"Yes. Yes I am. Here." She handed me an apron. "Are you ready?"

I tied on the apron, trying not to think about how domestic this felt. How right. "What if I mess up?"

"Then I'll fix it and we'll keep going. Let's do this?"

We started with the pumpkins. Isla demonstrated how to halve and gut them, her hands quick and sure, narrating each step in that teaching voice she used with Maple. I watched, trying to memorize the process, definitely not thinking about how close we were standing.

"Your turn." She handed me a knife.

I cut into the pumpkin, and—thanks to YouTube tutorials—I actually did it right. Clean cuts, seeds scooped out with minimal mess.

Isla paused mid-reach for the baking sheet. "You're doing well."

"Thanks." I transferred the pumpkin to the sheet. "How's this?"

"Good. Really good, actually." She looked at me with something like surprise. "You're taking this seriously."

"Of course I am. This matters to you." I brushed pumpkin seeds into the compost bin. "Plus Maple's been coaching me. She has very strong opinions about proper cookie decoration. It involves a lot of glitter."

"She has strong opinions about everything. It's quite entertaining. She asked me yesterday if I was going to be her teacher forever."

My hands stilled. "What did you tell her?"

"That I hoped so." She turned away, sliding the pumpkin into the oven. "Twenty-five minutes at 400. While that roasts, we'll prep the dough."

Her phone buzzed. She ignored it.

"You can answer that," I said.

"It's just another custom order. I'll deal with it later." She pulled flour from the pantry, set it down harder than necessary. "I've got four orders due Monday that I haven't started. But teaching you to decorate ghosts seemed more important right now."

"When's the last time you took a day off?"

"Day off?" She laughed, but there was no humor in it. "What's that?"

"Isla."

"I'm fine. Just busy. Fall's the busiest season. Well, maybe Christmas is busier." She measured flour, avoiding eye contact. "We should focus. If you handle the pumpkin roasting, I'll prep the spice mix. Then we can tag-team the dough and decorating."

"Sounds good."

She taught, I assisted, and we fumbled through the process like two people learning to dance who kept stepping on each other's feet. The pumpkin roasted, filling the bakery with that sweet-earthy smell. The dough came together under our hands, and somewhere between measuring spices and rolling out cookies, the nerves settled into something easier.

We worked well together. That was the surprising part. She'd start to reach for something and I'd already have it. I'd mess up a measurement and she'd fix it before I could apologize.

"Okay," Isla said after we'd rolled out the third batch of dough. "Now comes the part you've been dreading. Decoration."

"I'm not dreading it. I'm just... pre-accepting failure."

"That's the spirit." She pulled out piping bags and icing. "Remember—gentle pressure, steady hand, don't squeeze like you're angry at the bag."

"The bag and I have an understanding. It knows what it did."

She demonstrated on a cookie—clean lines, perfect curves, a ghost face that actually looked like a ghost. Then she handed me the bag.

I positioned it over my cookie, took a breath, and squeezed.

The ghost came out... not terrible. Lopsided, sure, and the eyes were probably too close together, but it was recognizably a ghost.

"Hey." Isla leaned in to examine it. "You've gotten better at this."

"Been practicing. Maple has wanted to practice every time she gets home from school." I added a mouth, which promptly looked demented. "Though apparently I still can't do mouths."

"Mouths are hard. Try making it smaller." She moved next to me, her shoulder brushing mine as she guided my hand. "Like this. Gentle curve."

Her hand over mine felt warm, her fingers steadying the bag as we piped together. The ghost's mouth came out crooked but charming, and I was definitely not thinking about how close she was or how she smelled like vanilla and cinnamon.

"There." She stepped back, leaving cold air where she'd been. "See? You can do this."

"Only with supervision."

"That's what I'm here for." She picked up her own piping bag.

My cookies got progressively less awful, and her instructions got more relaxed, less like she was teaching a particularly slow student and more like we were collaborators.

"Look at those," she said with a grin a few minutes later. She'd already finished hers and was watching me do my last couple. "They're charmingly imperfect."

"Charmingly imperfect. I'm putting that on my résumé."

By the time we finished, the kitchen was covered in flour and icing, and we both looked like we'd been through a small baking war.

Isla pulled off her apron, surveyed the damage. "Thank you for your help today. We got a lot done."

"Even though you had to hold my hand the entire time?"

She rolled her eyes. "There was no hand holding. You did great."

"I had an excellent teacher." That made her roll her eyes again.

She reached up to push her hair back, got flour on her face instead—a streak across her cheekbone that caught the kitchen light.

Without thinking, I reached up and brushed it off.

We both froze.

My thumb was still against her cheek, her skin warm under the dusting of flour. Her eyes went wide, and I watched her throat work as she swallowed. The kitchen suddenly felt smaller, the air warmer, the space between us microscopic.

Time did that thing where it slows down and speeds up at the same time. Her breath caught. My hand stayed raised, fingers barely touching her skin. I could count her eyelashes from here, could see the exact moment her gaze dropped to my mouth.

Her phone rang.

The spell broke. We both jerked back, the moment shattering like dropped glass.

"I should—" She grabbed her phone, didn't answer it. "That's probably the order from earlier."

"Right. Yeah." I stepped back, putting proper distance between us. "I should go anyway. Let you get back to work."

"Okay." Her voice came out unsteady. "Thanks again, Sawyer."

"Of course." I grabbed my jacket, trying not to look at her flushed cheeks or the way she was gripping the counter like it was the only thing keeping her upright. "And Isla? Thanks for not giving up on me. With the baking thing."

"Unfortunately, I don't give up easily." She met my eyes, and the weight of that statement settled between us. "See you tomorrow?"

"I'll be there."

I left before I could do something stupid like tell her I'd been thinking about how big an idiot I'd been for leaving her. Before I could admit that coming back to Acorn Field Heights was supposed to be temporary until I figured out what to do next, but every day I spent in her bakery made temporary feel less appealing.

The October air hit me cold and sharp, clearing my head. Main Street was dark except for the jack-o'-lanterns on stoops and the warm glow from the few houses still awake. Somewhere, a dog barked. Elsewhere, a screen door slammed.

I drove home with the windows down, letting the night air carry away the flour smell and the memory of her skin under my thumb. Aunt Caroline was knitting in a chair and told me in a low voice that Maple was asleep when I got home. Sure enough, Maple was sprawled across her bed with about fifteen stuffed animals and the ghost dog book she'd been reading all week.

I stood in her doorway watching her sleep, this perfect small person who trusted me completely despite all evidence that I had no idea what I was doing. The mediation was too soon.

Chapter Six

ISLA

The kitchen in my parents' house still smelled the same as it did when I was a teenager—cilantro and garlic, with the lingering scent of my mother's favorite vanilla-scented candles fighting against the spices. Some things never changed, including the way my mother bustled around the kitchen, batting away my attempts to help.

"I've got this." She waved a wooden spoon at me. "You work too hard already."

"Cooking isn't work for me, Mama. You know that." I leaned against the counter anyway, watching her add tomatoes to a simmering pot.

"I heard the bakery's been busy," my father said, entering the kitchen with his reading glasses perched on his nose. "Dolores mentioned you're entering the baking competition for the Fall Festival. That's great!"

"It's nothing special." I shrugged, aiming for casual. "I'm only entering it because it has a cash prize." One, I didn't mention, that would help me afford another person on the team.

"And Sawyer Thatcher has been hanging around the bakery, I hear." My father removed his glasses, folding them carefully before setting them on the counter. "Dolores said you two looked rather... comfortable together."

The way he said Sawyer's name—clipped, distasteful—made my stomach knot.

"He's helping me." I straightened my shoulders, fighting the urge to fidget like a teenager being reprimanded. "His daughter loves to bake."

"Ah yes, his child." My father's mouth tightened. "The one he had with another woman."

I blinked at the sudden venom in his voice. "Maple. Her name is Maple, and she's five."

"Five?" My mother paused her stirring, exchanging a look with my father. "So he wasted no time moving on after leaving, then."

My throat tightened. "It's not like that," I said, though I wasn't sure what I was defending. "Sawyer's a great dad. He's doing everything he possibly can for her, and it doesn't help that his ex-wife is threatening custody. I've just been entertaining Maple while he's figuring things out and—"

"You're spending a lot of time with him." My father's eyes narrowed. "After everything."

"I'm helping with his daughter," I corrected. "She's innocent in all this."

My mother shook her head, abandoning the stove to take my hands in hers. "Isla, we're just worried. That boy broke your heart once. Why put yourself in position for him to do it again?"

"I'm not—" I stopped, taking a breath. "It's not like that. I'm just helping with Maple."

"Sweetheart." My father's voice softened, which somehow made it worse. "We watched you rebuild after he left. You went to culinary school. Built your business. Made something of yourself, just like we'd always hoped."

"And I couldn't have done those things if he'd stayed?"

"You know how it is with boys like that," my father said. "Small-town dreams. Never would have left the farm. And you would have stayed with him, given up everything for him."

"You don't know that."

"Don't I? You were ready to follow him anywhere. Give up your

41

scholarship to stay close to him." My father leaned forward. "His leaving was the best thing that could have happened to you."

"The best thing?" I stared at him, something cold settling in my stomach. "You think him abandoning me without explanation was the best thing?"

"Oh, there was an explanation," my mother muttered, turning back to the stove.

The kitchen went silent. Even the pot seemed to stop bubbling for a moment.

"What does that mean?" I looked between them. "What explanation?"

My father cleared his throat. "Your mother means that his actions explained everything. He left because he wanted something else. Someone else."

But that wasn't what she meant. I could tell by the way she wouldn't meet my eyes, by the sudden tightness in my father's jaw.

"You know," I said slowly, taking a step towards her. "You know why he left."

"Doesn't matter now. Dinner's ready," my mother announced too brightly. "Get the plates, would you, Isla?"

"What did you do?" The question came out barely above a whisper.

My father sighed. "Isla, it was seven years ago. What does it matter now?"

"What did you do?" I repeated, louder this time.

"Nothing that wasn't for your own good." He straightened his shoulders. "That boy wasn't good enough for you. Never would be. I simply helped him see that."

The room tilted sideways. "You... what?"

"Your father merely pointed out some realities to the boy," my mother said, setting down a steaming platter. "About your future. His future."

"What realities?" My voice sounded strange in my ears. "What exactly did you point out to him, Dad?"

"That he would hold you back." My father's voice hardened. "That you deserved better than being a farmer's wife."

"You had no right—"

"I had every right," he cut me off. "I'm your father. It's my job to protect you, even from your own poor choices."

"By lying to me?" My hands trembled. "By making me think he just... just woke up one day and decided he didn't want me anymore?"

My mother touched my arm. "Isla—"

I jerked away. "What did you say to him? What did you do?"

The silence stretched, both my parents looking anywhere but at me.

"I asked him what he could offer you," my father finally said. "What future he could provide. If he truly loved you, he'd want what was best for you."

Something in his tone, in the careful way he chose his words, told me there was more. Much more.

"There's something you're not telling me." I pushed back from the table. "What else is there?"

My father's jaw worked. "Sit down, Isla. Dinner's getting cold."

"Suddenly, I don't have an appetite." I grabbed my purse. "I want to know what you did."

"It doesn't matter now," my mother pleaded. "It's in the past."

"Not to me it isn't." I headed for the door. "Not when I spent seven years thinking he just stopped loving me."

"Isla!" My father called after me. "Where are you going?"

I paused in the doorway. "To get the truth. Since I clearly can't get it from you."

The door slammed behind me, the sound echoing in the quiet street. I fumbled with my phone, hands shaking so badly I could barely scroll to Sawyer's name.

He answered on the second ring. "Hey."

"Where are you?"

His voice dropped when he responded. "Isla? Everything okay?"

"No," I said, voice cracking. "I need to talk to you. Now."

"I'm at home with Maple." His voice dropped. "What's wrong?"

"My parents. They said... I think they..." I couldn't form the words. "I need to see you. Please."

A pause. "Okay. You know where we're staying?"

"Asher mentioned the duplex on Elm."

"Number twelve. The one with the crooked mailbox." Another pause. "Isla... are you sure you're okay to drive?"

No, I wasn't sure of anything. "I'll be there soon."

Ten minutes later, I stood on the doorstep of a small duplex, porch light flickering. Before I could knock, the door swung open, revealing Maple in pink pajamas covered in unicorns, her hair damp from a bath.

"Miss Isla!" She bounced on her toes. "Did you bring cookies? Are you having a sleepover? I have extra unicorn pajamas! Daddy! Miss Isla is here!"

"I see that, jellybean," Sawyer appeared behind her, hair rumpled, wearing a faded t-shirt and jeans. His gaze searched mine, concern evident. "Hey."

For a moment, I just stared at him. This man who I'd spent seven years hating. Seven years believing had thrown away everything we had without a backward glance.

"I need to talk to you." My voice didn't sound like my own.

Sawyer nodded, clearly reading something in my expression. "Maple, can you go upstairs and pick out a bedtime story? I need to talk to Miss Isla for a minute."

"But I want to stay with Miss Isla!" Maple protested.

"I need to talk to your daddy," I said, gentling my tone. "Grown-up stuff. I promise it won't take long."

Maple's lower lip protruded. "Promise?"

"Cross my heart," Sawyer said, drawing an X over his chest.

She considered this, then nodded solemnly. "Okay. But I'm picking the longest story."

"Deal," Sawyer said, ruffling her hair. "Now scoot."

We watched her trudge up the stairs, dragging her stuffed unicorn behind her.

"Kitchen's this way," Sawyer mumbled, leading me through a living room stacked with moving boxes. "Sorry about the mess. We're still unpacking."

I barely registered the apology, my mind a hurricane of questions and accusations. The kitchen was small but clean, dishes drying in a rack beside the sink. Sawyer gestured to a chair, but I remained standing.

"What happened?" he asked, voice low enough that Maple wouldn't hear from upstairs. "You sounded upset on the phone."

I took a deep breath. "My father. Did he... did he do something to make you leave seven years ago?"

Sawyer went very still, color draining from his face. For a long, terrible moment, he didn't speak. Then, "Why would you think that?"

"He did, didn't he? Oh, that's just..." I said, my voice rising despite my effort to keep it down. "My parents let something slip at dinner. They said you leaving was the best thing for me, that my father 'pointed out some realities' to you."

Sawyer ran a hand through his hair, turning to stare out the window over the sink. "Isla..."

"Just tell me what happened. Please. I need to know why you left me. I thought... I thought you loved me and then you were just gone."

His shoulders slumped. "Isla... I—"

I took a step forward, closing into his space. "Please Sawyer. Please."

He sighed, tilting his chin up to stair at the ceiling before dropping his heavy gaze back to me. "Your father came to me and asked what I was thinking, pursuing you. He pointed out I didn't have my life together. That I had nothing to support you with. At that point, the farm was in trouble because Levi had taken over for my dad, and things were stressful. He... He told me that if I loved you, the best thing I could do was let you pursue your dreams. To let you go and not weight you down with my... lack of everything."

I gripped the back of a chair to steady myself. "He told you to leave me."

"Yeah, and..." Sawyer bit his lip, frowning. "He offered me money."

"How much?" I whispered.

Misery etched in every line of his face. "Twenty thousand dollars."

"And you took it?" The words tasted like ash.

"Yes." He nodded once. "I took it and gave it straight to Levi. It kept the farm running when I left. That was part of the deal, and it saved my family's farm. I'm so sorry, Isla. It was a stupid mistake, but one I couldn't undo once I took it."

"You just... You left."

Sawyer sank into a chair, looking suddenly exhausted. "Your father came to the farm and told me you'd gotten into that fancy culinary program in New York."

"I was going to defer," I said. "We talked about it."

"He knew that. Said you were throwing away your future for me." Sawyer stared at his hands. "Said I'd drag you down. That if I really loved you, I'd let you go."

"That wasn't his decision to make," I said fiercely. "Or yours."

"I know that. I was eighteen and terrified. My dad had his heart attack. The farm was struggling. Your father said..." He swallowed. "He said you'd wake up one day and realize I wasn't enough. That you'd resent me for holding you back. And eventually, you'd leave me anyway."

I sank into the chair opposite him, legs suddenly too weak to hold me. "And you believed him?"

"I believed I wasn't good enough for you," he corrected. "I always knew that. Your father just... confirmed it."

Seven years of anger and hurt crystallized into something new—a rage so pure it left me breathless.

"So you just left," I said. "Without a word. Without giving me a choice."

"You have to believe me when I say that I thought I was doing the right thing." His voice cracked. "Your father said you'd be better off without me. That I'd just be an anchor around your neck."

"And what about what I wanted?"

Sawyer reached across the table, then stopped, his hand falling short of mine. "I'm sorry, Isla. I know that doesn't fix anything. But I am so, so sorry."

I stared at his hand, at the calluses and small scars from farm work. The same hands that had once held mine. The same hands that now braided his daughter's hair and helped her decorate cookies.

"I don't know what to do with this," I admitted, my voice barely audible. "I spent seven years hating you. Building a life to prove I didn't need you. And now I find out it was all based on a lie?"

"Not all of it," he breathed. "You did build something amazing. Your bakery, your life here—that's real. That's yours."

"But the reason behind it..." I trailed off, overwhelmed.

Above us, floorboards creaked as Maple moved around her room. Life continuing while mine felt suspended between what I'd believed and what was true.

"Are you going to be okay?" Sawyer asked.

I shook my head, unable to form an answer. "I don't know."

And I didn't. Seven years of certainty had just crumbled beneath my feet, leaving me standing on nothing but confusion.

"I'll answer whatever questions you have, but I need to get Maple to bed." He stood, running a hand through his hair. "Will you be here when I come back down?"

I glanced up at him, my mind still racing. "I... I don't know."

"I understand. And Isla, I'm sorry."

I left before he came back down.

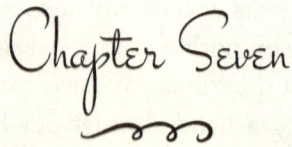

Chapter Seven

ISLA

As if my life couldn't get any worse, the next day at the bakery was chaos. I hadn't slept at all, and because of the dinner and the disaster, I hadn't had the evening to prep. The town was starting to fill with tourists because Acorn Field Heights took fall seriously, so there were more people than normal. By the time the afternoon rush hit at two-thirty, Sawyer arrived right in the middle of the chaos.

The line stretched to the door. I had cookies that needed to come out of the oven. And the commercial mixer—my beautiful, expensive, absolutely essential commercial mixer—was making a grinding sound that meant nothing good.

"Please, please, please," I muttered at it, hitting the power button again. The grinding got louder, then stopped entirely. The mixer went silent and still.

I stared at it, my vision going blurry at the edges. I couldn't afford to replace this. The repair alone would probably cost more than I'd made this week. And without it, I couldn't keep up with orders. Without orders, I couldn't—

"Isla?" Sawyer's voice cut through my spiral. "You okay?"

I hadn't heard him come in through the back. Maple stood beside him, already pulling off her jacket.

"The mixer's dead." My voice came out too high. "I can't—I don't know what—"

"Let me look at it."

"You don't have to—"

"Farm equipment breaks the same way bakery equipment does." He was already rolling up his sleeves. "Give me ten minutes."

I wanted to argue, but a customer was calling from the front about her order, and another was asking about gluten-free options, and everything was falling apart at once.

I handled the customers while Sawyer disappeared behind the mixer with a screwdriver from my emergency toolkit. Maple planted herself at the register and started greeting people with enthusiasm.

"Welcome to the magic cookie place!" she announced to a confused tourist. "My daddy's fixing the broken machine because he's really good at fixing things. Miss Isla makes the best cookies in the whole world. Would you like to try one?"

The tourist, charmed despite himself, bought three dozen cookies.

By the time I boxed his order, Sawyer had the mixer running again. The grinding sound was gone, replaced by the smooth hum I'd been taking for granted for three years.

"Just a loose belt," he said, wiping his hands on a towel. "Should be fine now. But you might want to have someone check the motor soon."

I stared at him, then at the mixer, then back at him. "You just saved me about two thousand dollars and possibly my entire business."

"It was just a belt."

"It was—" My throat closed. I turned away before he could see my eyes getting wet. "Thank you."

I didn't know how to feel. For one, I was mad at my parents, and rightfully so. I was also mad at Sawyer for even listening to my father, let alone taking the bribe to leave me. But also, I couldn't help but understand the insecurities my father had preyed on. And I believed Sawyer when he apologized and said he regretted it. I didn't know what to think about the whole thing, but there was a part of me that had filled with relief at the sight of him.

The afternoon rush continued, but with Sawyer there, it felt manageable. He'd gotten good at this—boxing orders, making change, handling the customers who had seventeen questions about ingredient sourcing. A woman with twin toddlers asked about the difference between our sugar cookies and our snickerdoodles, and Sawyer explained it perfectly.

"Your helper is wonderful," the woman said to me as she left, twins clutching cookie bags. "So patient with children."

I watched Sawyer clean the counters. He was good at this. Not just helpful—actually skilled. He remembered regular customers' names, knew which cookies sold out fastest, could work the register without asking for help.

When had that happened? When had "Sawyer sometimes helps out" become "Sawyer is essential to my afternoon operations"?

We closed at six, and Maple was passed out in the window booth, her coloring book still open on the table. Sawyer carried her carefully to his truck while I locked up.

"Same time tomorrow?" I asked.

"If you need me. Though I should probably warn you—after tomorrow, I might not be much good to anyone. I really need to figure this custody thing out."

"Sawyer—"

"Only a handful of days." He adjusted Maple in his arms. "Keep thinking maybe if I say it enough times, it'll stop feeling like a countdown to losing everything."

I wanted to promise it would be okay. That the mediator would see what I saw—a father who showed up, who tried, who loved his daughter with everything he had. But promises felt dangerous when the stakes were this high.

"I'll see you tomorrow morning," I said instead. "Early. I need help with the bread before you have to go to the farm."

Something in his face shifted. "You sure?"

"I'm sure."

"And are you... Are you okay?"

I sighed, then nodded once. "I'm fine."

After they left, I stayed in the bakery longer than necessary, reorganizing shelves that didn't need organizing and making lists I'd probably never use. The mixer hummed quietly in the corner, fixed by someone who I used to love.

I pulled out my phone and opened my notes app. Typed: *Need to hire full-time help. Can't keep doing this alone.*

I stared at the words for a long time before closing the app and heading home.

Sawyer showed up at five-thirty on Tuesday morning, moving quietly through the back door like he was worried about waking the building.

"You're early," I said, already elbow-deep in bread dough.

"Couldn't sleep. Figured I might as well be useful." He washed his hands and joined me at the worktable.

"Why?"

"Jen's coming soon. She wants to see Maple, which I know in my head makes sense. She's her daughter too, but she's the one who wanted a divorce. I mean, she's the one who left. It feels unfair, and I'm stressed out of my mind."

We fell into the rhythm we'd been building—me shaping loaves while he prepared the pans, both of us moving around each other in the small kitchen space without collision. The ovens warmed the air, and outside the windows, Main Street was still dark and quiet.

"When's she coming?" I asked.

"Ten tomorrow. Her and the lawyer both." He pressed a loaf into its pan with more force than necessary. "Levi's making sure the farm looks perfect since we stayed there for a while. Asher's helping by making sure anything that might look dangerous is hidden. I unpacked most of the boxes, at least of Maple's stuff. And I'm going to stand there and pretend my hands aren't shaking while my ex-wife and her lawyer decide if I'm competent enough to raise my own daughter. Then the actual mediation is the first day of the festival. But I'm still afraid it's not enough."

"You are competent. More than competent."

"Tell that to Jen. She keeps saying Maple needs stability. Structure.

A real home. And that I need a real job that doesn't include shoveling horse manure." He set the pan down too hard, flour puffing up from the work surface. "Maybe she's right. Maybe I'm kidding myself thinking I can—"

"Stop." I grabbed his wrist, stopping him mid-reach for another pan. "You're spiraling. I can hear it. You're playing out the worst-case scenario in your head."

"Because that's what's going to happen. She's going to take Maple to Portland, and I'll become the weekend dad who drives three hours each way and pretends seeing his daughter for forty-eight hours every two weeks is enough."

"That's not going to happen."

"You don't know that."

"I know you love Maple more than anything. I know she's happy here. I know you've built something real in three months." I squeezed his wrist before letting go. "That has to count for something."

We finished the bread in silence, loading the ovens and setting timers. Sawyer checked his phone every few minutes, his jaw getting tighter each time.

"I should go," he said at seven-thirty. "Get the farm ready. Get the house ready. Make sure everything looks—" He stopped. Started over. "I don't even know what I'm supposed to make it look like. What does a proper home look like to someone who already decided I'm not good enough?"

"Like yours. Like Maple's drawings on the fridge and her boots by the door and her toothbrush in the bathroom. Like life." I walked him to the back door. "And Sawyer? Whatever happens tomorrow—you're not alone in this."

He looked at me for a long moment, something complicated crossing his face. "I should never have asked you to get involved. With my mess. With—"

"Too late. I'm involved. Are you—" I stopped myself, but he raised an eyebrow and waited. "Are you coming to the Harvest Moon Dance tonight?"

Despite everything he smiled. "Yeah. I'll see you there."

After he left, I tried to focus on the morning rush, but my mind kept drifting to the farm. To Jen arriving with her lawyer and her demands and her version of what was best for Maple. To Sawyer trying to defend a life he'd barely started building.

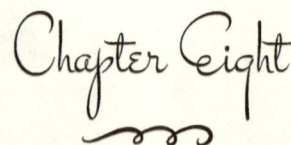

Chapter Eight

SAWYER

The harvest moon hung low and orange over the village green, casting everything in amber light that made the world look like it had been dipped in honey. I stood at the edge of the gazebo, watching couples move in slow circles to the fiddle music, and tried not to think about tomorrow. About Jen arriving with her lawyer. About the way Maple had asked three times if Mommy was going to take her away.

"Daddy, look!" Maple tugged on my hand, pointing to where a group of kindergarteners were playing ring-around-the-rosy near the refreshment table. "Can I go play?"

"Stay where I can see you."

She was already running, tutu bouncing, before I finished the sentence. I watched her join the circle, her laugh carrying over the music. She looked happy. Normal. Like a kid whose world wasn't about to potentially implode.

"She seems to be doing well."

I turned. Isla stood behind me in a dark green dress that made my brain temporarily forget how to form words. Her blonde hair was down for once, falling in waves past her shoulders, and she'd done something with her eyes that made them look bigger, greener. The bakery apron and flour-dusted jeans were gone, replaced by someone who looked like she'd stepped out of a painting.

"You look—" I stopped, tried again. "That dress is—"

"Thank you." A smile played at the corner of her mouth. "You clean up pretty well yourself."

I'd actually ironed my shirt. Found my one pair of dress shoes that weren't work boots. Even attempted to tame my hair, though that had been a losing battle from the start.

"Dance with me?" The words came out before I could think them through.

She hesitated, and I thought she might say no. Then she took my hand.

The gazebo floor was crowded with couples, but somehow we found space. My hand settled on her waist, hers on my shoulder, and we moved into the simple two-step that everyone in Acorn Field Heights learned before they could properly walk. She smelled like vanilla and cinnamon, like the bakery, but also something else. Something floral and soft that made me want to pull her closer.

"You're nervous," she said after a moment.

"That obvious?"

"Your shoulders are practically at your ears." She shifted her hand, thumb pressing gently at the tension. "Tomorrow?"

"Yeah." I guided us through a turn, using the movement to check on Maple. Still playing, still laughing. "What if I missed something? What if they they decide the farm was an unsafe place for Maple to live? What if—"

"It will be fine."

"You don't know that."

"I know you." Her hand squeezed mine. "I know how much you love Maple. How hard you're trying. That has to count for something."

The song ended, transitioning into something slower. Couples adjusted, moving closer. I should have let go, stepped back, maintained the safe distance we'd been dancing around. Instead, I pulled her closer.

"Can we not talk about tomorrow?" I asked. "Just for a little while?"

"What do you want to talk about?"

"Are you okay? After everything with your parents?"

She stiffened slightly in my arms. "I'm managing."

"That's not what I asked."

"I know." She was quiet for a moment, her fingers tightening on my shoulder. "I'm angry. At them. At you, a little, still. At myself for not seeing it. For spending seven years building my whole identity around being the girl who got left behind."

"Isla—"

"But I'm also relieved." She looked up at me, eyes bright in the moonlight. "Because now I know. The story I'd been telling myself wasn't the whole truth. You didn't just wake up one day and decide I wasn't worth it."

"You were always worth it. Worth everything."

"I know that now." Her voice dropped. "And for what it's worth, I forgive you. For listening to him. For leaving. For all of it."

Something tight in my chest loosened. "Really?"

"Really. You were eighteen and scared and someone you respected told you leaving was the loving thing to do." She shook her head. "I hate that my father did that. I'm sorry. I'm so sorry he manipulated you like that."

"It's not your fault."

"I know, but I still feel responsible somehow." She bit her lip. "He had no right to make that choice for us."

The music swirled around us, violin and fiddle weaving together into something sweet and mournful. Other couples moved past; Mayor Goldwin with his wife, my brother Asher dancing awkwardly with Quinn from the costume shop, Levi and Amberlyn looking like they were having an entire conversation without words.

"I should have fought for you," I said. "Should have told your father exactly where he could put his money and his opinions."

"We were kids. We did the best we could with what we knew." She rested her forehead against my chest for a moment, and I felt her breathe. "I just wish we hadn't lost so much time."

I glanced over at Maple, now attempting to teach her friends some elaborate dance that seemed to involve a lot of spinning. Seven years. Seven years of mistakes and different paths and choices that had led us here, to this moment, dancing under the harvest moon while my daughter, the only thing in my life that wasn't a mistake, played nearby.

"Maybe we needed it," I said. "The time apart. To become who we are now."

Isla pulled back enough to look at me. "You really believe that?"

"I don't know. But you built your bakery. I have Maple. Those things wouldn't have happened if we'd stayed together back then."

"True." She was quiet for a beat. "Though I would have liked the chance to choose."

"Yeah."

The song was ending, but neither of us moved to separate. Around us, couples were breaking apart, heading for the refreshment table or to collect children. But Isla stayed in my arms, and I wasn't ready to let go.

"Daddy!" Maple's voice broke the spell. "Madison's mom brought cookies!"

I looked down to find my daughter tugging on my pants leg, her face bright with excitement and probably sugar.

"Did you already have one?"

"Maybe." She held up three fingers. "This many."

"That's three, jellybean."

"I can count!" She noticed Isla then, eyes going wide. "Miss Isla! You look like a princess! A real one, not a pretend one!"

"Thank you, sweetheart." Isla smoothed Maple's hair, which had mostly escaped from the braid I'd attempted earlier. "You look pretty magical yourself."

"I know. Daddy said I'm the prettiest girl here, but I think you are." She grabbed Isla's hand. "Come see the cookies! There are ghost ones and pumpkin ones but yours are better."

"Maple, Miss Isla might want to—"

"It's fine." Isla squeezed my hand once before letting Maple pull her toward the refreshment table. "I should inspect the competition."

I watched them go, Maple chattering about cookie decoration while Isla listened with genuine interest. The sight did something complicated to my chest, made me think dangerous thoughts about the future. About possibilities.

"You've got it bad."

I turned to find Asher standing beside me, hands in his pockets, trying to look casual despite the fact that his shirt was obviously new and he'd actually styled his hair.

"Says the guy who ironed his jeans for Quinn Fairchild."

"They're not ironed. They're just clean." He watched Isla and Maple at the cookie table. "Maple seems to love her."

"Yeah."

"And you?"

I didn't answer, but apparently my face did it for me.

"Oh man." Asher shook his head. "You're done for. Again. Does she know?"

"Know what?"

"That you're completely gone for her. That you're probably already imagining Sunday dinners and shared holidays and Maple calling her mom."

"I'm not—" I stopped. Tried again. "It's complicated."

"It's really not." He clapped me on the shoulder. "Just don't mess it up this time."

He wandered off, probably to find Quinn, leaving me standing alone at the edge of the dance floor. The band was taking a break, and people were milling around, voices mixing with children's laughter and the distant sound of owls. The October air had a bite to it now, making everyone cluster closer to the heat lamps someone had set up.

I found Isla and Maple near the gazebo steps. Maple was demonstrating some kind of complicated hand game she'd learned at school, and Isla was trying to follow along, laughing when she got the pattern wrong.

"I'm going to play with Madison more," Maple announced. "Is that okay?"

"Sure. Make sure one of your uncles or Mimi Caroline are nearby."

She ran off again, energy apparently inexhaustible despite the sugar crash that was definitely coming later. Isla and I stood there in sudden silence, aware that we were alone in a crowd.

"Walk with me?" I asked.

She nodded, and we drifted away from the gazebo, toward the darker edges of the green where the lamplight barely reached. The noise of the dance faded behind us, replaced by the rustle of leaves and our footsteps on grass.

"Thank you," I said. "For forgiving me. For understanding. For everything with Maple."

"You don't have to keep thanking me."

"I do, though. You didn't have to—" I stopped walking, turned to face her. "After everything, you could have told me to get lost. Could have turned Maple away. But you didn't."

"I could never turn Maple away. She's—" Isla paused, choosing her words carefully. "She's impossible not to love."

"Just Maple?"

The question hung between us, loaded with seven years of history and two months of careful dancing around what was happening now. Isla looked up at me, moonlight catching in her eyes, and I saw the moment she made a decision.

"No," she whispered. "Not just Maple."

I moved first, or maybe she did, or maybe we both did. But suddenly she was in my arms and I was kissing her, really kissing her, for the first time in seven years. She made a soft sound against my mouth, her hands coming up to frame my face, and the world narrowed to just this—the taste of cider on her lips, the warmth of her body against mine, the way she kissed me back like she'd been waiting for this as long as I had.

It was sweet and desperate and careful all at once. An apology and a promise and a question rolled into one moment that stretched and contracted like time had forgotten how to work properly. Her fingers curled into my hair, and I pulled her closer, trying to memorize everything—the way she fit against me, the small sigh she made when we broke apart for air, the way her eyes stayed closed for a heartbeat after.

"I've wanted to do that since the first day we walked into your bakery," I admitted.

"Just that first day?" Her voice was teasing, but breathless.

"Every day. Every minute. Every time you smiled at Maple. Every time you got flour in your hair. Every time you handed me a piping bag and told me to try again."

She kissed me again, softer this time, sweeter. Like we had time. Like tomorrow wasn't looming with its lawyers and evaluations and the possibility of losing everything.

"We should get back," she said against my mouth. "Maple will wonder where you went."

"Yeah."

Neither of us moved.

"Sawyer?"

"Hmm?"

"I'm glad you came home."

"Me too," I agreed.

We walked back to the gazebo hand in hand, not caring who saw, not caring what people would say. Dolores was definitely already composing the group text that would have the whole town talking by morning. But right now, with Isla's hand in mine and Maple's laughter carrying across the green, I felt something I hadn't felt in years.

Hope.

Tomorrow would come with all its threats and challenges. But tonight, under the harvest moon that Mayor Goldwin swore made promises binding, I was choosing to believe that maybe, just maybe, everything would be okay.

Chapter Nine

SAWYER

The high from kissing Isla lasted exactly eleven hours and twenty-three minutes. Right up until Jen's rental car pulled into the duplex's driveway at ten on the dot, her lawyer in the passenger seat, both of them wearing expressions that meant business.

Maple pressed her face against the window, watching them approach. "Is Mommy going to be nice today?"

"Of course she will be." I straightened her collar, tried to smooth down the stubborn cowlick that always stuck up at her crown. "Remember what we talked about? Just be yourself."

"But what if myself isn't good enough?"

The question gutted me. I crouched down to her level, taking her small hands in mine. "You are more than enough. You're perfect exactly as you are."

She didn't look convinced, but the doorbell rang before I could say more.

Jen stood on the porch in an expensive navy suit, her dark hair pulled back in a way that made her look older, sharper. The lawyer beside her—a thin man with wire-rimmed glasses—carried a tablet and a folder thick with what I assumed were all the ways I was failing as a parent.

"Jennifer," I said, because calling her Jen felt too familiar now.

"Sawyer." Her gaze moved past me to Maple. "Hi, baby."

"Hi, Mommy." Maple's voice was small, uncertain.

Jen's professional mask slipped for a moment, something soft crossing her face. Then she straightened, and the mask was back. "Shall we start with the tour?"

The next hour was excruciating. Jen and her lawyer—Mr. Davidson —walked through the duplex like they were documenting a crime scene. He took photos of everything. The cluttered living room I hadn't finished unpacking. The small kitchen with its outdated appliances. Maple's room, which at least looked good thanks to Asher helping me assemble her furniture and Isla dropping off fairy lights she said were extras from the bakery.

"Just one bathroom?" Mr. Davidson noted something on his tablet.

"It's sufficient," I said.

"And the lease? Month to month?"

"For now. The landlord's willing to do a year lease once—" Once I figured out my life. Once I proved I could afford it. "Soon."

Jen picked up one of Maple's drawings from the coffee table—the one of us at the bakery with Isla. Her jaw tightened almost imperceptibly before she set it down.

The farm was next. Levi had everything running like a Swiss watch, the barn immaculate, the equipment properly stored. He came out to greet us, professional and friendly in a way that would have been funny if I wasn't so stressed.

"The environment seems a bit dangerous for a child," Mr. Davidson observed, gesturing at the tractor.

"Maple knows the safety rules," I said. "She doesn't go near equipment without supervision."

"But accidents happen on farms," Jen added. "Heavy machinery, animals. It's not exactly child-friendly."

I wanted to point out that thousands of kids grew up on farms without incident. In fact, my brothers and I had been just fine. Besides, Maple loved the animals and had learned responsibility helping with the chickens. But I kept my mouth shut, knowing everything I said would be twisted into evidence against me.

The kindergarten visit was marginally better. Maple's teacher, Mrs. Ries, gushed about what a delight she was, how well-adjusted, how creative. She showed Jen the reading corner where Maple liked to curl up with books, the art wall featuring her drawings, the progress reports showing she was ahead in most areas.

"She's thriving here," Mrs. Ries said, and I could have hugged her for the conviction in her voice.

But Jen just nodded, taking notes on her phone, giving nothing away.

After the kindergarten, we stood in the parking lot in awkward silence. Maple was back in class, and I felt her absence like a missing limb.

"We'll be in touch about next steps," Mr. Davidson said, shaking my hand with a firm grip.

"Actually," Jen said, "I'd like to talk to Sawyer alone for a moment."

The lawyer looked surprised but nodded, heading to the car. Jen waited until he was out of earshot before turning to me.

"She looks happy," she murmured.

"She is happy."

"For now. But what happens when you can't make rent? When farm work isn't enough? When you have to move again?" She crossed her arms. "I'm not trying to be cruel, Sawyer. I'm trying to be realistic."

"I'm figuring it out."

"You're always figuring it out. That's the problem." She sighed, and for a moment she looked like the woman I'd married—tired, frustrated, but not unkind. "I want what's best for her."

"So do I."

"Then prove it. Show me you can provide stability. Real stability, not just good intentions and borrowed time." She moved toward the car, then paused. "The mediation's on Saturday. If you can't show substantial changes by then..."

She didn't finish. She didn't need to.

After they left, I sat in my truck for ten minutes, hands shaking too hard to drive. Everything Jen had said was true. The duplex was too small. The farm job barely covered expenses. I was one bad month from having to move again.

I needed air. I needed to move. I needed to do something with the panic clawing at my chest.

I drove to the bakery.

Isla was in the middle of the lunch rush, hair escaping from her bun, flour streaked across her cheek, juggling three orders while the phone rang. She looked up when the bell chimed, and whatever she saw on my face made her expression shift.

"Kitchen," she said. "Now."

"You're busy—"

"Anna, watch the front," she called to a customer who apparently was a regular. The older woman nodded, moving behind the counter like she'd done it before.

Isla grabbed my hand and pulled me through to the kitchen, where the familiar smell of baking bread and the warm, close air felt like stepping into safety.

"How bad?" she asked.

"They documented everything. The small duplex. The month-to-month lease. The farm being dangerous." I slumped against the counter. "Jen said I need to prove stability. Real stability."

"You're stable. You have a job, a home, Maple's in school—"

"The farm job isn't enough. We both know that. And Levi can barely afford to pay me as it is because he's been buying up all the real estate before that development company can." I rubbed my face, exhaustion hitting like a wall. "I need to find something else. Something that looks better on paper."

Isla moved closer, her hand coming to rest on my arm. "It'll work out."

"You don't know that."

"I know you. You don't give up. Especially not when it comes to Maple."

She was standing close enough that I could see the faint circles under her eyes, the way her shoulders carried tension even when she was trying to comfort me. The lunch rush was still happening in the front, orders piling up, and here she was, taking time she didn't have to talk me off a ledge.

"I should let you get back to work," I said.

"Work can wait."

"No, it can't. You're drowning out there."

"I'm managing."

"Barely." I straightened, falling into the easier rhythm of helping rather than being helped. "What needs doing?"

"Sawyer—"

"Let me help. Please. I need to do something useful or I'm going to lose my mind."

She studied me for a moment, then nodded. "Okay."

"Okay." I washed my hands, tied on an apron, and got to work.

We fell into the rhythm we'd been building over the past two weeks. I handled the register and boxing orders while Isla caught up on the baking. Anna stayed to help for another hour, the three of us managing to get through the lunch rush without anyone complaining about wait times.

When things finally slowed around two, Anna left with a box of pastries Isla insisted she take. The bakery was quiet except for one couple in the corner sharing a cinnamon roll.

"Thank you," I said, pulling off the apron.

"You're the one who helped me." Isla was restocking the display case, not looking at me.

"Not just for letting me help. For taking my mind off things. For—" I stopped, unsure how to put into words what it meant that she'd seen me falling apart and had thrown me a lifeline without making it feel like charity.

She turned then, and before I could overthink it, before I could talk myself out of it, I crossed the space between us and pulled her into a hug.

She stiffened for a moment, surprised, then melted against me, her arms coming around my waist. We stood there in her kitchen, holding on to each other while the ovens cooled and the afternoon sun slanted through the windows.

"It's going to be okay," she murmured against my chest.

"You keep saying that."

"Because I need to believe it too."

I pulled back enough to look at her. There was flour in her hair and exhaustion in her eyes and something soft and fierce in her expression that made my chest tight.

"Last night—" I started.

"Was perfect," she finished. "Don't overthink it."

"I'm not. I just—with everything happening—"

"I know. The timing is terrible. Your life is complicated." She reached up, her palm resting against my cheek. "But we've already lost seven years. I don't want to lose any more time being careful."

I leaned into her touch, closing my eyes. "I don't want to hurt you again."

"Then don't."

It sounded so simple when she said it like that. Like I could just choose not to hurt her, choose to stay, choose to make this work despite everything stacked against us.

The bell over the front door chimed. More customers. Isla stepped back, the moment breaking.

"I should go get Maple from school soon," I said.

"Bring her by after? She can color while I prep for tomorrow."

"You sure?"

"Always."

I wanted to kiss her. Wanted to pull her back into my arms and forget about lawyers and mediation and the countdown ticking in my head. But customers were waiting, and life didn't stop for wanting.

"I'll see you in a bit," I said.

She nodded, already moving toward the front, slipping back into her professional smile.

I left through the back door, stepping into the October afternoon that felt too bright, too normal for everything that was falling apart.

Chapter Ten

ISLA

A day had passed since Jen's initial visit, and Sawyer looked like he'd aged two years. He moved through my kitchen on Wednesday afternoon like a ghost, mechanically rolling dough while Maple colored at her usual table. Dark circles shadowed his eyes, and his shoulders carried a tension that made me ache just looking at him.

"Any luck with the job search?" I asked, though his expression already gave me the answer.

"Nothing that pays enough to matter." He shaped a loaf with more force than necessary. "The hardware store's not hiring. Neither is the grocery. Erickson's garage might have something next month, but that doesn't help me now."

"Maybe—"

"Nobody's hiring." His voice was flat. "I need to prove I can provide stability here, where Maple's happy."

From the corner, Maple hummed while she colored, occasionally looking up at us with those too-perceptive eyes. She'd been quieter since her mother's visit, clinging closer to Sawyer, asking repeatedly when she'd see Mommy again.

"Mommy called this morning," Maple announced suddenly, as if she'd heard us thinking about her. "She said I'm staying with her this weekend."

Sawyer's hands stilled on the dough. "She did?"

"She said it would be fun. That we'd go shopping and get our nails done." Maple didn't sound excited. She sounded worried. "But I told Mommy I normally have baking class with Miss Isla on Saturdays."

"I have the festival this Saturday, princess. We were going to have to reschedule anyways," I said.

"But I don't want to reschedule." Her lower lip trembled. "I want to stay here and make cookies and help Daddy and play with the barn cats."

Sawyer crossed to her in three strides, pulling her into his arms. "It's just for the weekend, jellybean. You'll have fun with Mommy."

"But what if she doesn't bring me back?"

Sawyer's face crumpled for just a moment before he pulled it back together. "She'll bring you back. I promise."

"Pinky promise?"

He linked his pinky with hers, but I saw the uncertainty in his eyes. The fear that he couldn't actually keep that promise.

The bell over the front door chimed. Three customers entered, tourists from the look of them, cameras around their necks and that slightly lost expression people got when navigating small towns.

"I've got it," Sawyer said, already moving toward the front.

I watched him shift into customer service mode—smile in place, voice friendly but tired. He'd gotten good at this, learning the rhythms of the bakery, the regular orders, which cookies sold best at different times of day. He moved like he belonged here.

The thought should have been comforting. Instead, it terrified me.

While he handled the customers, I sat down next to Maple. "You okay, sweetheart?"

She shrugged, a gesture too world-weary for a five-year-old. "Daddy's sad. He thinks I don't know, but I do. He's scared Mommy's going to take me away."

"Your dad loves you very much."

"I know." She looked up at me with those serious eyes. "That's what Mommy said. That Daddy loves me but can't take care of me properly."

Rage, hot and sudden, flashed through me. What kind of mother said that to a child?

"Your daddy takes excellent care of you," I said, fighting to keep my voice even. "Look at you. You're happy, healthy, doing great in school. You have friends, a home, people who love you. That's what proper care looks like."

"Will you tell that to the meadow-ator?"

"The mediator?"

"That's what I said."

"I would if I could, sweetie."

She went back to coloring, adding purple clouds to what appeared to be a bakery floating in the sky. I returned to the kitchen, mind racing. Three days until the mediation. Sawyer still didn't have a better job. His ex was already taking Maple. The walls were closing in, and I didn't know how to help.

My phone buzzed. A reminder about the Fall Festival baking competition. The same day as the mediation. The ten-thousand-dollar prize that would let me hire help so I could keep giving Maple her happy place and—

No. I couldn't plan on winning. That was magical thinking, not practical planning.

But still.

I pulled up the competition requirements on my phone. Three categories: presentation, taste, and creativity. I'd been planning a three-tier autumn harvest cake with maple buttercream and spiced apple filling. Good, but not spectacular. Not ten-thousand-dollars spectacular.

"What are you plotting?" Sawyer had returned, the tourists gone with their boxes of cookies.

"The baking competition. I need to win."

"You will."

"You don't know that." I showed him my sketches. "This is good, but good doesn't win. Spectacular wins. And I'm too tired to be spectacular."

He studied the sketches, head tilted. "What if you added sculpture work? Like, made leaves out of sugar? Or marzipan pumpkins?"

"I don't have time to—"

69

"I could help. I've gotten decent at decoration, thanks to Maple's intensive training." He attempted a smile. "If I can't find a job in the next three days, at least I can help you win that competition."

"Sawyer—"

"Please." His voice cracked. "Let me be useful. It's the only thing keeping me sane right now."

Before I could respond, the bell chimed again. But this time it wasn't customers.

Jen stood in the doorway, dressed in jeans and a sweater like she was trying to look casual but still managed to seem like she was heading to a corporate retreat. Her gaze swept the bakery, taking in Maple at her corner table, Sawyer in his apron, me with flour in my hair.

"Mommy!" Maple jumped up but didn't run to her. "What are you doing here?"

"I came to see you, baby. And to talk to Daddy." Her eyes fixed on Sawyer. "Can we speak privately?"

"We can talk here," he said, not moving from beside me.

"Fine." She stepped closer, lowering her voice but not enough that I couldn't hear. "I've been talking to my lawyer. Sawyer, are you even trying to find a job? If you don't have stable employment by the mediation—"

"I know."

"Do you? Because from where I'm standing, you're playing baker's assistant while our daughter's future hangs in the balance."

"I'm working on it—"

"Will you be making enough to cover rent? Health insurance? School expenses?" Jen's voice stayed calm, reasonable, which somehow made it worse. "I'm not trying to be cruel. This isn't sustainable."

"And taking her to Portland is?"

"I have a job there. A real job with benefits and stability. A good school district. A two-bedroom apartment where she'd have her own room."

"She has her own room here."

"In a month-to-month rental you can barely afford."

They stared at each other, years of history and hurt between them. I wanted to intervene, to point out that Maple was happy here, thriving here. But this wasn't my fight. Not technically.

"I'm taking her through Sunday evening," Jen said finally. "My lawyer says it's within my rights as her mother."

"She told me. Would've been nice to hear it from you first, though." Sawyer kept his tone even, but beneath his words lay a thin line of hurt. "It's fine. I know you haven't seen her in a while."

"I haven't. Thank you for understanding. But Sawyer? If things don't change by Saturday..." She trailed off, but the threat was clear.

After she left, the bakery felt smaller, like the walls had moved in a few inches. Maple hadn't returned to her coloring, standing instead between the counter and her table like she didn't know where she belonged.

"Come here, sweetheart," Sawyer said, and she ran into his arms.

"I don't want to go with her," she whispered, but we all heard it.

"I know. But it's just for the weekend."

"You keep saying that."

He had no response. Neither did I.

———

I hadn't seen Sawyer in two days.

Two days of running the bakery alone, burning a batch of croissants when my timer failed, and smiling at customers when all I wanted to do was close early and check if he was okay. But I didn't. Because checking meant admitting how much I already needed him around, and that felt dangerous when Dolores had just told me the news.

"He's been asking around in Bridgeport," she'd said that morning, leaning across my counter. "My cousin works at the machine shop there. Said Sawyer came in yesterday asking about positions."

Bridgeport was forty minutes away. Not Portland-far, but far enough that daily visits would become weekend visits. Far enough that whatever we'd started would stretch and thin until it snapped.

"Maybe he was just exploring options," I'd said, trying to keep my voice neutral while boxing Dolores's usual order of lemon scones.

"Maybe." But her tone suggested she didn't believe it any more than I did.

Now it was Thursday afternoon, and the bakery felt wrong without Maple's chatter from the corner table. Without Sawyer's steady presence in the kitchen, remembering which customer liked extra cinnamon, which preferred their cookies slightly underbaked. The corner table sat empty except for the small stack of coloring pages I'd printed out of habit.

The bell chimed, and my traitorous heart jumped. But it was just Mrs. Patterson, here for her Thursday apple turnover.

"Seems quiet in here," she observed, looking around.

"Just a slow day."

"Hmm." She paid exact change, took her box, and paused at the door. "Sawyer found work yet?"

"I wouldn't know."

"Really? Because the whole town seems to think you two are—"

"Have a nice day, Mrs. Patterson."

She left with a knowing look that made me want to flip the sign to closed and hide in my kitchen until everyone forgot about Sawyer and me and the mess we'd made of trying to find our way back to each other.

My phone buzzed. A text from Amelia Avery, Amberlyn's mother, of all people.

> Coffee? I have a business proposition.

I almost said no. The last thing I needed was to discuss business when I couldn't focus on my own work. But the bakery was empty, and sitting alone with my thoughts felt worse than pretending to be professional.

> Sure. Here or the cafe?

> I'll come to you. Be there in ten.

She arrived in eight. Her hair was pulled back neatly, her sweater didn't have flour stains, and she definitely hadn't been up since three a.m. stress-baking.

"Thanks for meeting," she said, settling at the counter. "I'll get straight to the point. I know my daughter talked to you about a collaboration. We're interested in extending it, and I wanted to see if you shared the same interest. Exclusive partnership. You get premium product at wholesale rates, we get a reliable buyer and cross-promotion opportunities."

"That's... brilliant."

"It was Amberlyn's idea." She smiled. "Plus it helps both our businesses. Win-win."

"When would this start?"

"Whenever you're ready. Though I'd suggest we announce it at the festival. Maximum visibility."

"That works."

Amberlyn's mother studied me. "Are you okay? You seem distracted."

"Just tired. You know how it is, running a business alone."

"Actually, about that." She pulled out her phone, scrolled to something. "I might know someone looking for part-time work. My sister's friend just moved back to town, has restaurant experience—"

"I can't afford to hire anyone." The admission came out sharper than intended. "I mean, thank you, but my margins are too thin right now."

"What about after the festival? If business picks up?"

If I won the contest. If Sawyer stayed. If, if, if.

"Maybe," I said.

Amelia nodded, but something in her expression suggested she saw through my deflection. "Can I ask you something? Not about business?"

"Okay?"

"Is Sawyer really looking for work outside town?"

I stared at her. "How did you—never mind. Dolores?"

"Dolores," she added, a small smile crossing her face. "It would be a shame if he had to leave again. I think we've all been happy to have him back. It was the same when Asher returned."

73

"Yeah," I tucked a strand of hair behind my ear, unsure what else to say.

"Are you doing okay?"

I didn't answer, couldn't figure out how to explain that I was watching the same story play out again—Sawyer leaving because circumstances demanded it, me left behind to pretend I hadn't built hope on someone who couldn't stay.

"He's doing what he has to," I said finally. "For Maple."

"And you're protecting yourself by pulling back."

"I'm not—" I stopped. Because I was. I hadn't texted him in two days. Hadn't offered to help with the job search. Hadn't done anything except wait and hurt and guard my heart like it wasn't already too late.

"I think my daughter did the same thing with Levi when she initially came back. Kept one foot out the door, ready to run if things got hard. She's in Boston now deciding if she's going to come home for good or not."

"This is different. Sawyer has a child. A custody battle. Real reasons he might have to leave."

"Real reasons you could fight for him to stay."

Before I could respond, the bell chimed again. This time it was Sawyer.

He looked exhausted—hair rumpled, stubble past the point of intentional, wearing the same red flannel I'd seen him in three days ago. But his eyes lit up when he saw me, and my stupid heart did that thing where it forgot I was supposed to be protecting it.

"Hey," he said.

"Hey."

Amelia looked between us, then stood. "I should go. Think about the partnership, Isla. And..." She glanced at Sawyer. "Think about the other thing too."

She left, and suddenly the bakery felt too small, too quiet, too full of everything we weren't saying.

"I've missed you," Sawyer said finally.

"You knew where to find me."

"I didn't think you'd want—I've been dealing with things. The job search."

"I heard. Bridgeport?"

His face fell. "How did—Dolores. Of course." He moved closer to the counter. "I'm sorry."

"Sawyer, you know I can't think about you losing Maple. It would break my heart. It terrifies me to think about her being taken away from you. And... and think about you leaving to follow her."

"I wouldn't—"

"You would. If she went to Portland, you'd follow. Don't pretend otherwise."

He was quiet for a long moment. "You're right. I would."

The honesty of it hurt more than a lie would have.

"But," he continued, "I'm going to fight to make sure that doesn't happen."

"And if it's not enough?"

"I... I don't know."

I rolled my lips inward and nodded once. "Right."

"I'm sorry."

"I know you are."

Chapter Eleven

SAWYER

"I'm sorry, Lee." I set the pitchfork against the barn wall, unable to meet my brother's eyes. "I know this leaves you in a bad spot."

Levi leaned against the stall door, arms crossed, that particular expression he got when he was trying not to show how stressed he was. "It's fine. I'll figure it out."

"It's not fine. Harvest season's starting, you need the help, and I'm bailing on you."

"You're not bailing. You're trying to keep your daughter." He pushed off from the wall, clapped me on the shoulder. "Family first. Always."

"This is family too."

"Yeah, but Maple's five. The farm will survive without you. She won't."

I wanted to argue, to point out that the farm was barely surviving *with* me, but my phone rang before I could. Unknown number.

"Hello?"

"Mr. Thatcher? This is James Milton from the college."

Hope flared. "Yes?"

"I'm calling about your inquiry regarding employment with the grounds staff. I'm afraid we don't have any positions available at this time."

The hope died. "Nothing? Not even part-time?"

"I'm sorry. Budget constraints, you understand. But we'll keep your application on file."

"Right. Thanks."

I hung up and found Levi watching me with sympathy. "Job inquiry?"

"Yeah. That's a no."

"What else have you tried?"

"You're not going to like it."

"You went forward with Eastbrook?"

I grimaced. "Yeah. I'm sorry. If it makes you feel any better, I haven't heard back, which is probably for the best. Can you imagine if I took a job with the company you've been fighting?"

"I'd understand. If it meant keeping Maple, I'd understand."

"Yeah, well, I doubt they'll want me anyway."

My phone rang again. This time it was Jen.

"What?" I answered, already defensive.

"Nice greeting. Maple's asking about a specific recipe? She said you'd know it. I think it has pumpkin or cinnamon or something." In the background, I heard my daughter crying, and my muscles tensed.

"Can you put her on the phone?" I asked, trying to calm myself down.

"She's not really in a talking mood."

"Jen, please?" There was silence for a second before a weepy Maple spoke.

"D-daddy?"

"Hey jellybean. Can you explain to me what you want to make and I'll tell Mommy?"

It took coaxing, but I eventually translated her five-year-old description into an answer.

"It's pumpkin creme brûlée," I told Jen, pinching the bridge of my nose. "She was practicing it last weekend with Isla."

"You're telling me our daughter knows how to make a French dessert?" Jen sighed. "Never mind. Thank you. I'll see you on Saturday."

The line went dead.

I stood there in the barn, phone still pressed to my ear, listening to nothing. Levi had turned away, giving me the illusion of privacy while I fell apart.

"I can't lose her, Lee," I said finally.

"What are you going to do?"

"Go to any interview I can find. Hope for a miracle. Try not to lose my mind."

I left the farm feeling like I'd abandoned my brother right when he needed me most. But I couldn't fix that. Couldn't fix anything except try to present myself as someone worth hiring at an interview for a job that might not matter anyway.

I drove to the bakery, needing to see her even if I had nothing good to report.

She was behind the counter when I walked in, and the way her face lit up then immediately shuttered told me Dolores had been busy spreading more news.

"How'd the interview go?" she asked, but her voice was careful. Distant.

"Fine. Good, maybe. They'll let me know."

"That's great."

"Is it?"

She turned away, busying herself with rearranging perfectly arranged cookies. "Of course it is."

"Isla."

"I'm working."

"The bakery's empty."

"I still have things to do."

I moved around the counter, stopping just out of reach. "What's wrong?"

"Nothing."

"Try again."

She spun to face me, and there was hurt in her eyes that made my chest tight. "Dolores told me you applied to a job in North Dakota. You've going to leave again and it's killing me."

"I told you, I need—"

"A job, I know. But you're already planning your exit strategy, aren't you?"

"That's not—I'm trying to stay—"

"By looking for work everywhere but here?"

"There's nothing here!" The words came out louder than intended. "I've tried everything. The hardware store, the grocery, the garage, Town Hall. Nobody's hiring. Nobody wants a single dad with a complicated history and no degree."

"I want you." Her voice cracked. "I—"

"I know, but I'm not going to be the dad that just disappears out of my daughter's life."

"I get that, I do, but Sawyer, I... I don't want to go through this again. I don't want to be here, watching you leave. I don't want to be hurt like that. I—I can't."

"That's not going to happen."

"Isn't it? Because from where I'm standing, you've got one foot out the door already."

"I'm doing what I have to for Maple."

"I know." She met my eyes, and the resignation there was worse than anger would have been. "And I have to protect myself. I can't—I can't do this again. Watch you leave. Make excuses for why it's necessary. Pretend it doesn't feel like dying."

"I'm not leaving you."

"You're not staying either. You're in between, trying to have both, and that's almost worse."

I crossed my arms and narrowed my eyes. "What do you want me to do? Give up? Let Jen take Maple?"

"No. I want you to—" She stopped, shook her head. "It doesn't matter what I want."

"It matters to me."

"Does it? Because you haven't asked. Ugh, and I know this all sounds incredibly selfish, because it is. But you... I... You've made all these decisions, looked for work everywhere, assumed you know what's best, but you haven't asked what I want. What I need."

"Fine. What do you need?"

She was quiet for a long moment. "I need someone who chooses to stay. Not because they have to, not because circumstances force it, but because they want to be here. With me. Building something together."

"I do want that."

"But you want Maple more. And you should. She's your daughter. She comes first." She turned back to her cookies. "I hate that this is so selfish. I feel awful. But that means I have to come second, or third, or wherever I fit in the list of priorities. And I understand that. I do. But I also have to protect myself."

"So what are you saying?"

"I'm saying you need to do what's best for your daughter. And I need to do what's best for me."

The words sat between us, final and terrible.

"That's it? We're done?"

"We never really started." Her voice was steady, but her hands shook as she adjusted the cookies again. "We were just pretending. Playing house with your daughter, acting like we could pick up where we left off. But we can't. Too much has happened. Too much has changed."

"I love you."

The words hung there, desperate and true and completely inadequate.

"I know," she whispered. "That's what makes this so hard."

I stood there for another moment, waiting for her to take it back, to say we could figure this out, to fight for us the way I was fighting for Maple. But she didn't. She just kept arranging cookies that didn't need arranging, not looking at me, armor fully in place.

I left because there was nothing else to do. No argument that would change the reality of our situation. No promise I could make that wouldn't potentially be a lie.

Outside, Main Street looked offensively normal. People shopping, kids playing, life continuing while mine fell apart in new and creative ways. Maple was with her mother until mediation. The woman I loved had just ended things before they'd really begun.

And I still didn't have a job that would matter to anyone making decisions about my daughter's future.

I sat in my truck, staring at my phone, willing it to ring with good news. A job calling to say I was hired. Jen saying she'd changed her mind. Isla texting to say she didn't mean it.

But the phone stayed silent, and the sun kept setting, and Saturday kept getting closer.

One day.

One day to figure out how to keep my daughter.

One day to accept that keeping Maple might mean losing Isla.

Chapter Twelve

ISLA

Friday morning arrived with overcast skies that matched my mood perfectly. The festival setup was supposed to start at seven, but I'd been at my booth since six-thirty, arranging displays.

"Need help?"

I looked up from the apple turnovers I was arranging. Aunt Caroline stood there with a steaming cup of coffee and that expression that meant she knew everything and had opinions about it.

"I'm fine."

"Sure you are." She set the coffee on my table—real coffee, not her usual bitter brew—and started helping me arrange pastries without being asked. "Saw Sawyer helping Levi set up their booth."

I focused on aligning the cookies perfectly. "Good for them."

"He looks about as fine as you do. Which is to say, terrible."

"Aunt Caroline—"

"I'm not meddling. Just observing." She adjusted one of my price cards. "Also observing that you're both idiots."

"Thanks. Really helpful."

"You pushed him away because you're scared."

"I pushed him away because he's leaving. Again. It's what he does."

"Is it? Or is it what circumstances force him to do?" She turned to face me fully. "That boy's been bending over backward trying to find a way to stay. Everyone in town knows it."

"Looking for work in Bridgeport isn't trying to stay."

"Looking for work that would let his daughter stay is exactly trying to stay." She softened her voice. "Honey, I know you're protecting yourself. But sometimes protecting yourself means you miss out on the very thing you're trying to save."

Before I could respond, the wind picked up, sending napkins flying. We both scrambled to catch them, and by the time we'd secured everything, more vendors had arrived. The noise level rose as people called greetings, hammered stakes, argued about booth placement.

Aunt Caroline left to set up her own booth, but not before squeezing my shoulder and giving me a look that said we weren't done discussing this.

The morning flew by in a blur of preparation. The weather grew increasingly ominous, clouds darkening from gray to nearly black. The wind kept gusting, threatening to tear down banners and send product flying. Everyone worked faster, trying to get things secured before the rain started.

I was adjusting my banner for the fifth time when I saw him. Sawyer was at the Thatcher Farms booth, helping Levi arrange produce. He looked exhausted—shoulders slumped, movements mechanical. He glanced my way once, our eyes meeting across the thirty feet between our booths, but he looked away quickly.

My phone buzzed with a weather alert. Severe thunderstorm warning starting at three p.m.

Of course. Because this day needed to get worse.

"Better cover everything," Mayor Goldwin called out, making rounds. "This one's looking nasty."

I pulled out the tarp I'd brought, thankful I'd thought ahead. Other vendors were scrambling, sharing supplies, everyone helping everyone else. The community coming together the way small towns did when weather threatened.

Sawyer appeared at my booth with bungee cords. "You need these more than we do."

"I have rope."

"Bungee cords work better in wind." He started securing one corner of my tarp without waiting for permission. "Learned that the hard way."

We worked in silence, him on one side, me on the other, the tarp whipping between us. His fingers brushed mine as we both reached for the same corner, and we jerked back like we'd been burned.

"Thanks," I said when we finished.

"Yeah."

He turned to go.

"Sawyer—"

But thunder cracked overhead, drowning out whatever I might have said. The rain started as he jogged back to his brother's booth—fat drops that quickly became a downpour.

Everyone ran for cover. Booth owners yanking last-minute items under tarps, visitors sprinting for their cars, kids shrieking with delight or terror depending on their age. Within minutes, the festival ground was empty except for the sound of rain hammering on canvas and metal.

I made it to my car as the sky truly opened up. The rain came so hard I couldn't see across the parking lot. I sat there, soaked despite the short run, watching the storm destroy all our careful preparation.

Tomorrow's festival might be ruined. The competition might be canceled. Everything we'd worked toward washed away like it never mattered.

But all I could think about was Sawyer's exhausted face and the way he'd still stopped to help me with my tarp.

I drove to the bakery through streets that were rapidly becoming streams. The storm was getting worse—branches down, debris flying, rain so heavy the wipers couldn't keep up. I made it to the bakery and parked in the back, then sat in my car for a moment, gathering the energy to run through the rain.

Inside, the bakery felt like a sanctuary. Warm, dry, smelling of yeast and cinnamon from this morning's baking. I had so much to do for tomorrow—if tomorrow even happened. The competition cake to finish, the backup stock to prepare, the impossible hope that somehow the weather would clear and the festival would go on.

I worked steadily through the afternoon and into the evening. The storm raged outside, thunder shaking the windows, lightning illuminating everything in stark flashes. The power flickered twice but held. I kept baking, kept preparing, because stopping meant thinking and thinking meant admitting how badly I'd handled everything with Sawyer.

By one o'clock in the morning, I was exhausted but not done. The three-tier cake for the competition sat half-assembled. Sugar work still needed to be completed. The detail work that might make the difference between winning and losing waited for hands steadier than mine currently were.

I was attempting to pipe delicate maple leaves when the knock came.

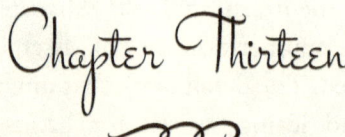

Chapter Thirteen

SAWYER

The storm woke me at 1 a.m. Wind rattled the windows hard enough that I thought the glass might shatter. Rain hammered the roof in waves that sounded like handfuls of gravel being thrown. I sat up, listening to the house groan under the assault, and something in my chest pulled tight.

My phone buzzed on the nightstand. Then again. And again.

I grabbed it. Six missed calls from Jen. Three voicemails. A cascade of texts, each one more frantic than the last.

> Maple's not in her room

> I can't find her anywhere

> She's not in the house

> CALL ME

My thumb hit her contact before I finished reading. She answered on the first ring.

"She's gone!" Jen's voice cracked, and I could hear her moving, hear doors opening and slamming. "I went to check on her because of the storm and her bed was empty and I've looked everywhere and—"

"How long?" I was already pulling on jeans with one hand, my phone pressed between my shoulder and ear.

"I don't know! I tucked her in at nine, but I fell asleep and when I woke up to check because the storm was so loud—" She made a sound like a sob catching in her throat. "Where would she go? In this storm? She could be—"

"Call Sheriff Marx." I grabbed my jacket from the hook by the door, my truck keys from the counter. My hands shook so badly the keys rattled. "Tell him Maple Thatcher is missing. He knows me. He'll help. I'm going to look for her. Stay there in case she comes back."

"Where would she—"

"I don't know yet, but I'm going to find her. I'll come to you first and search nearest there. On my way now." I hung up before she could say anything else, before the fear in her voice could wrap around my chest any tighter than it already had.

The storm antagonized me the second I stepped outside. Rain so hard it stung my face, wind that nearly knocked me sideways. I couldn't see my truck until I was three feet from it. Couldn't see the road when I backed out of the driveway. The windshield wipers fought a losing battle against sheets of water, and my headlights barely cut through the darkness.

At a stop sign, I paused and hit Levi's contact. It rang and rang. Nothing. He was probably asleep. Everyone was probably asleep. It was the middle of the night.

I tried calling again. Nothing. Tried Asher. Tried Aunt Caroline. The call wouldn't even connect. I glanced at my signal—one bar, then none, then one again before disappearing entirely.

"No, no, no." I hit redial three more times. Nothing went through.

The cell tower. It had to be the tower nearest town. The storm must have knocked it out.

I threw the phone into the passenger seat and pressed harder on the gas. Trees were down everywhere—across driveways, blocking side streets, one massive oak split down the middle and sprawled across someone's front yard. Power lines sparked in the distance, throwing brief flashes of blue-white light that made everything look like a nightmare.

And somewhere in this mess was my daughter. Five years old. Probably terrified. Definitely alone.

My throat went tight. I swallowed hard and focused on the road, on getting to Jen's place, on making a plan that didn't involve imagining all the ways this could end badly.

Jen was standing in the driveway of the rental when I pulled up, soaked through despite the raincoat she'd thrown on. Her hair was plastered to her face, and she looked nothing like the put-together woman who'd shown up in town last week wanting custody. She looked like I felt—wrecked and desperate and barely holding it together.

I didn't think. I just pulled her into a hug. Things were long since over between us, but our daughter was missing and I needed the hug as much as I assumed she did.

"I've been up and down the street," she said, choking out the words as I stepped back. "I checked the neighbor's yards, the park at the end of the block, everywhere I could think of within walking distance."

"Which direction?" I had to yell over the rain.

"Both! I went both ways! She's not here, Sawyer, she's not—"

I grabbed her shoulders. "Hey. Look at me." She did, her eyes wide and red. "We're going to find her. But we need a plan. You take north through town. Check the grocery store, the library, the gas station anywhere with an overhang where she might take shelter. I'll go south toward the farm and cover the main roads. We split up, we cover more ground."

"What if she's not—"

"She is." I said it with more confidence than I felt. "Our daughter is smart. She found somewhere safe. We just have to figure out where."

Jen nodded, wiping rain from her face with a shaking hand. "Why would she run? I mean, we argued about coming here. She wanted to go home with you, but I told her we'd watch a movie and make popcorn and—"

"I don't know, Jen. I don't know. Did you call Sheriff Marx?"

"I tried. Lines are jammed. Everyone's calling about the storm."

"Okay, new plan. Keep trying, but go to the station first. It's near the gas station. If you find her, call. Leave your door here unlocked in case she comes back. I'll call you when I find her."

"If you find her—"

"When." I squeezed her shoulders once more, then let go. "Get in your car. Start driving. Careful of the dirt roads. They turn to peanut butter in storms like this."

I watched her climb into her rental car, watched her taillights disappear into the storm, and then I was alone with the rain and the wind and the growing panic I couldn't let take over.

The farm. She loved the farm. Loved the animals, loved watching Levi work, loved climbing on the hay bales in the barn. If she'd run away, that's where she'd go first. Right? She certainly hadn't gone to the duplex, though I'd left the door unlocked just in case.

I drove faster than I should have, my truck hydroplaning twice on flooded sections of road. The turn onto Millstone Road was blocked by a downed tree—a huge maple that had taken out a section of fence with it. I had to reverse and take the long way around, adding ten minutes I didn't have.

When I finally made it to the farm, Levi's truck was gone.

My chest went hollow. The house was dark, no lights on anywhere. I ran to the porch anyway, pounded on the door, tried the handle even though I knew it'd be locked. The barn next—I splashed through puddles deep enough to soak my boots, yanked open the barn door and shouted her name into the darkness.

"Maple! It's Daddy! Are you here?"

Nothing. Just the sound of rain on the roof and a few startled animals.

I checked every stall, every corner, the loft where she liked to hide during games. Called her name until my voice went hoarse. She wasn't there.

Back in the truck, I tried my phone again. Still no signal. I slammed my palm against the steering wheel hard enough that pain shot up my arm, but the physical hurt was better than the tightness in my chest that made it hard to breathe.

Where else? Where would she go?

The school. She talked about her classroom all the time, about the reading corner with the bean bags and the art table by the windows. Maybe she'd gone there.

I drove through town, past storefronts with dark windows and streets running with water. The school parking lot was empty, the building completely dark. I tried the main entrance anyway—locked. The side door near the playground—locked. I ran around back to where the kindergarten classrooms had their own entrance, pulling on the handle so hard the door rattled in its frame.

Nothing.

The playground was next to the building, just a few swings and a small slide under a metal awning. I ran to it, checked under the slide, behind the equipment shed, anywhere a small body might fit.

"Maple!" Rain ran down my face, into my eyes, mixing with something that might have been tears. "Maple, please! It's Daddy!"

The wind threw my words back at me.

She wasn't here.

I stood in the middle of the empty playground, rain pounding down, and tried to think. Where else did she talk about? Where did she want to go?

Maybe the church. It was a long shot, but it was nearby. I ran back to the truck and drove the three blocks to the church, my hands gripping the wheel so hard my fingers went numb. The parking lot was flooding, water halfway up the curb. I parked and ran anyway, my boots splashing through water that soaked my jeans to the knee.

The church doors were locked. Both of them. I pounded anyway, shouted Maple's name, tried to peer through the narrow windows but couldn't see anything in the darkness.

She wasn't here either.

I sank down on the church steps, rain pouring over me, and tried to catch my breath. My chest hurt. My hands wouldn't stop shaking. Every second that passed was another second she was out there somewhere, cold and scared and alone.

Think. Where else? Where would a five-year-old go in a storm?

She loved the library, but it'd be locked too. The grocery store—closed at night. The park—Jen had already checked. Levi's house—

empty. Asher's place was clear across town, and she'd been there only once.

My phone buzzed.

I grabbed it so fast I nearly dropped it. One bar of signal. One bar was enough.

The screen showed a picture of Levi leaning against the barn with the time at the top. It was nearly 4am. I hit answer, pressed the phone to my ear.

"Lee?" I croaked, realizing only after I said my older brother's name that I was crying. "Finally. Cell tower went down, I couldn't reach anyone—Maple's gone. She ran away from Jen. I've been looking for three hours and I can't find her anywhere, and with the storm—"

"Hey, take a deep breath." Levi's voice was calm. "Where have you looked?"

"Everywhere. The house, the barn, the fields. Jen said they fought about going home and Maple just ran into the storm three hours ago. She's five and she's been out there for three hours—"

"Have you checked the bakery?"

I hadn't. The words fell out of my mouth as I took a minute to process his question. "The bakery?"

"Isla's place. You guys have been spending a lot of time there. Maple talks about it constantly."

"I—no. I didn't even think—" The bakery. She had to have gone there. But if it was locked... I leapt to my feet and splashed through the growing pond in the church parking lot towards my truck. "I'm maybe ten minutes out."

"We're ninety minutes away. We'll help when we get there." Levi's voice was still steady. "Call the second you know anything."

I yanked open my truck door and closed it behind me. It was still running from when I'd left it. "Tower's still spotty but I'll try. Thank you—"

The line went dead before I could say more. Probably the tower again. I didn't have time to think about where my brother was or why he'd said "we" or anything else except trying to get to the bakery.

I threw my phone onto the passenger seat and jammed the truck into reverse. The bakery was only ten minutes away. Ten minutes and I'd know. Ten minutes and she'd be safe. She had to be safe. I sent a prayer that Levi was right.

I made it five minutes before my truck hit mud.

The back road that cut through to Main Street was more river than road now, water rushing across in a current strong enough to push debris against the sides. I tried to power through a section that looked shallow—it wasn't. The truck's rear wheels spun, caught, spun again, and then sank.

No. Not now. Not when I was this close.

I threw it in reverse. The wheels screamed and went nowhere. Forward. Nothing. Reverse again. The truck rocked but didn't move.

"No!" I hit the steering wheel again and ground my teeth. My daughter needed me. I turned the truck off, grabbed my phone and shoved it in my jacket pocket. I bailed out into the storm, locking my truck behind me. Water immediately soaked through my already wet jeans, and cold mud sucked at my boots with every step. I didn't care. The bakery was maybe half a mile ahead. I could run that.

I ran.

Rain pelted my face, wind tried to push me sideways, and my boots slipped in the mud with every other step. My lungs burned. My legs felt like lead. But I kept going because somewhere ahead was my daughter and I had to get to her. Had to know she was okay. Had to see her safe.

Main Street appeared through the rain—storefronts dark except for one. The bakery. Lights on in the windows, warm and bright against the storm.

I ran harder, my boots pounding against pavement now, and didn't slow down until I reached the door. I pressed my face to the glass, cupping my hands around my eyes to block the glare.

The front room was empty. Just tables and chairs and the display case. No Maple. No one.

My heart dropped.

"No." I banged my fist against the door, rattling the handle. It was locked. "No, no, no—"

I pounded harder, using both fists. "Isla!" The sound barely carried over the thunder and wind. "Isla, please!"

Nothing. Just my reflection in the glass and the empty bakery beyond.

I hit the door again, desperation clawing up my throat. "Isla! It's Sawyer! Please!"

Movement flickered in the back doorway. A shadow crossed behind the counter, and then Isla appeared, her eyes going wide when she saw me. She rushed forward, fumbling with the lock.

The door swung open and I stumbled inside, dripping and shaking.

"Is she here?" The words tore out of me. "Is Maple here? Please tell me she's here."

"Yes." Isla grabbed my arm. "Yes, she's in the back—"

"Daddy!"

Maple burst through the doorway behind the counter, her hair damp but drying in waves around her face. She wore an oversized sweater that hung past her knees—Isla's, probably. Her little feet were bare except for fuzzy socks that were too big and bunched at the ankles.

She ran straight at me.

My knees hit the floor and I caught her as she crashed into my chest. My arms wrapped around her small body, holding her so tight I worried I might hurt her, but I couldn't let go. Couldn't stop shaking. Couldn't breathe past the sob that ripped out of my throat.

"You're okay." The words came out broken. "You're okay, you're safe, you're here."

"I'm sorry, Daddy." Her voice was muffled against my soaked jacket. I could feel her tears soaking through the wet fabric. "I was so scared of the storm and I just wanted you and I didn't know what to do so I ran and—"

"Shh, it's okay." I pulled back just enough to see her face, my hands cupping her cheeks. I had to make sure she was real. That she was here. That she wasn't hurt. "Are you hurt? Did you fall? Did anything hit you?"

She shook her head, tears streaming down her face. "I'm sorry. I didn't mean to make you scared."

I pulled her close again, pressing my face into her damp hair, and the sob I'd been holding back finally broke free. My shoulders shook with it.

Three hours of searching. Three hours of imagining the worst. Three hours of thinking I might never hold her again.

"I was so scared," I whispered against her hair. "I looked everywhere for you. I thought—" My voice cracked and I couldn't finish.

"Don't cry, Daddy." Her small hands came up to my face, trying to wipe away tears. "Please don't cry."

But I couldn't stop. Not yet. The relief was too big, too overwhelming. She was safe. She was here in my arms where she belonged.

A hand settled gently on my shoulder. I looked up to find Isla kneeling beside us.

"She showed up around two in the morning," Isla whispered. "She showed up soaking wet and terrified. I got her into dry clothes and let her rest in the back room. I tried calling, but the lines are down. I was going to bring her to you as soon as the storm broke. You know how the roads get. I didn't want to risk them."

"Thank you." My voice came out raw. "I can't—thank you."

"Of course." She squeezed my shoulder. "She's safe. That's what matters."

Maple pulled back slightly, her hands still on my wet face. "Your face is all wet, Daddy."

"It's just rain," I managed.

She wiped at my cheeks with her oversized sleeves. "And tears. You're crying."

"Yeah." I tried to smile. "Yeah, I am. Because I love you so much and I was so worried about you. You can never run away again, jellybean. Ever."

"I won't." She pressed her forehead against mine. "Can we go home now? I want to go home."

"My truck got stuck. We're going to have to wait," I said, glancing at Isla. "Is that alright?"

She nodded and rose to her feet. "That's fine. If you want to try to sleep, the booth over there is—"

"I won't be able to sleep, but," I said, turning to Maple, the relief starting to fade and reality slipping back in. "You go lie down."

"But—"

"Now Maple," I nudged her towards the booth. "I need to call your mommy. Or at least try."

Maple dragged her feet all the way to the booth, but after Isla turned out the lights in the front, I checked ten minutes later and my daughter was already sleeping.

In the back of the bakery, I ran a hand through my wet hair and tried to steady myself. All of the adrenaline I'd been channeling for the last three hours seeped out of my bones, and I felt unsteady on my feet. Isla must've noticed because she pointed me towards a stool.

"She's safe, Sawyer," she said softly. "You can breathe again."

"I know," I said, rubbing my face. "I know." And even though I did know, one last shock of panic slipped through my mind and silent tears streamed down my cheeks. I pressed the heels of my hands into my eyes, startling when a second later, warmth wrapped around me in a hug. I fell apart in Isla's arms.

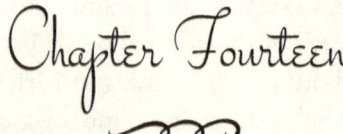

Chapter Fourteen

ISLA

I held Sawyer while he fell apart. His shoulders shook under my hands, silent sobs wracking through him as he sat hunched on the stool in my bakery's back room. I didn't say anything. Didn't try to comfort him with empty words. Just kept my arms around him and let him break.

The storm had gentled outside, rain pattering against the windows instead of hammering. The worst had passed. Maple was safe, curled up in the front booth wrapped in a blanket I'd grabbed from the back of my car. But Sawyer was still shaking, still soaking wet, still crying, and my chest ached watching him.

"I'm sorry," I whispered against his wet hair. "Sawyer, I'm so sorry."

He pulled back, wiping his face with the back of his hand. His eyes were red and swollen. "For what? You kept her safe. You—"

"Not for that." I sat on the stool next to him, close enough that our knees touched. "For this week. For being distant. For making everything harder when you're already dealing with so much."

"Isla, you don't have to—"

"Yes, I do." I took his hand, cold and still trembling. "We argued about you leaving and I was selfish. I got scared and I pulled away instead of talking to you about it. And tonight, when Maple showed up, I couldn't even call you because the tower was down. You were out there searching and I couldn't tell you she was safe and—" My voice cracked. "I'm sorry."

Sawyer turned his hand over, lacing his fingers through mine. "You have nothing to apologize for."

"Neither do you. You're doing everything you can for Maple. Fighting for custody, looking for stable work, trying to build a life for her. I know that. I've always known that." I squeezed his hand.

"Maple doesn't want to leave, and neither do I," he whispered. "I want to stay here with you and her and build something together. But if I lose custody—"

"You won't."

"You don't know that."

"No, but I know you. I know how much you love her. Any judge who sees you two together will know it too. You just risked your life driving around searching for her in the middle of one of the worst storms I've seen in years. And she wasn't running away from you." I reached up and wiped a remaining tear from his cheek. "You're a good father, Sawyer. The best."

His throat worked as he swallowed. "I was so scared tonight. I thought—" He stopped, shaking his head.

"I know." I pulled him close again, and this time his arms came around me too. "But she's safe. You found her. That's what matters."

We stayed like that for a moment, wrapped around each other in the dim light of my bakery's back room. The smell of sugar and cinnamon hung in the air, mixing with the earthy scent of rain and mud lingering on him. Outside, the storm continued its gentle fade toward dawn.

Sawyer's phone buzzed in his pocket. He pulled back, checking the screen. "One bar. Finally." He stood up, moving toward the back door where the signal might be stronger. "I need to call Jen. Let her know Maple's safe. Levi and Asher too."

I nodded and started pulling ingredients for the competition cake I needed to finish. The baking competition started in—I checked the clock—six hours. I'd been up all night with Maple, but exhaustion would have to wait. I had a cake to finish and a competition to win.

Behind me, I heard Sawyer's voice, low and rough. "Jen? Yeah, I found her. She's at the bakery... No, she's fine. She's sleeping... I know. I know you were scared too... My truck's stuck in the mud. Soon as the roads clear and I can get it out, I'll bring her to you... Yeah. Okay. I'll call you in a few hours."

He hung up and came back to stand beside me. "Jen's at the sheriff's station. She's been trying to get help organizing a search party."

"How is she?"

"About as wrecked as I am." He rubbed his face. "What are you doing?"

"Finishing my entry for the competition." I measured out icing sugar, my hands steady despite the exhaustion pulling at me.

"You've been up all night."

"So have you." I glanced at him. "Do you want to help me?"

"I might ruin it."

"I doubt that." I handed him a mixing bowl. "Start mixing this icing sugar with the butter there."

He took the bowl, and something in his expression softened. "Okay."

A little while later, I covered a yawn with my hand. "Coffee. I need coffee. Do you want some?"

"I'll make it." He set down the piping bag he'd been preparing and moved to my industrial coffee maker. "Where's the—"

"Second cabinet on the left."

He found the coffee and started a pot brewing while I finished with the sugar maple leaves. The back room filled with the rich smell of coffee mixing with cinnamon and sugar, and for a moment, everything felt almost normal.

Sawyer poured two mugs and handed me one. "Thank you. For tonight. For keeping Maple safe. For—" He gestured vaguely at the baking supplies around us. "For this."

"You don't have to thank me." I took a sip of coffee, letting the heat seep into my exhausted bones. "I love Maple. And I—" I stopped, the words catching in my throat.

"You what?"

I glanced up at him through my lashes. His hair was still damp and messy, his clothes rumpled and stained with mud. He looked exhausted and wrecked and handsome, and I couldn't keep pretending I didn't feel what I felt.

"I love you," I whispered. "I know it's complicated and you're dealing with custody and maybe moving away, but I love you. And I'm tired of being scared of that. Seeing you love your daughter so fiercely even though you might lose custody made me realize that I shouldn't stop loving you just because you might leave. It means I should love you more."

Sawyer set down his coffee mug. Took two steps and pulled me into his arms.

When we pulled apart, he rested his forehead against mine. "I love you too. The mediation is today. After that, I'll know what I'm fighting for. But whatever happens, I want to do it here. With you."

The oven timer went off, breaking the moment. I pulled away reluctantly and grabbed oven mitts. "Help me get these cinnamon rolls out and iced. Then you need to check on Maple."

"I should leave by six-thirty to drop off Maple, then get cleaned up and pick up some decent clothes from my place." He glanced down at his muddy jeans and soaked jacket. "Can't show up looking like I wrestled a swamp."

"Probably not the impression you want to make."

We fell back into silence as I finished assembling and decorating the cake. Sawyer watched, occasionally handing me tools or steadying the cake stand when I needed both hands. By the time dawn broke through the bakery windows, the cake was done.

"It's beautiful," Sawyer said.

"It's tired baking." I stepped back, surveying my work with a critical eye. "But it'll do."

Outside, the rain had stopped completely. Early morning light filtered through the clouds, turning everything soft and gold. The storm was over.

Sawyer checked his phone. "Roads should be clearing. I should try to get my truck out."

"I'll drive you." I grabbed my keys. "Maple can sleep in my car until you get it unstuck."

We woke Maple gently. She was groggy and quiet, leaning against me in the front seat while Sawyer climbed into his truck and tried the engine.

It took twenty minutes of rocking back and forth, but finally the truck pulled free from the mud with a sucking sound. Sawyer stuck his head out the window, grinning.

"Got it!"

I transferred Maple to his truck, buckling her in while she mumbled sleepily about wanting pancakes. Sawyer walked me back to my car, and I handed him a paper box from the bakery.

"What's this?"

"Cinnamon rolls. For you and Maple." I touched his hand. "Good luck at mediation. You're going to do great."

He leaned in and kissed me softly on the forehead. "Thank you. For everything. I'll call you after?"

"You better."

I watched him drive away, Maple's sleepy face visible through the window. Then I drove back to the bakery, where my competition cake waited and the morning shift would start in an hour and life would go on.

The festival grounds looked like a war zone. Booths knocked over, banners torn, debris scattered across the village green. But the community had turned out in force, everyone helping everyone else rebuild what the storm had destroyed.

I parked near what used to be my booth and climbed out, surveying the damage. My display case had shattered. The awning was in pieces. But the structure itself was salvageable, and several people were already working to right it.

"Isla!" Mayor Goldwin waved from across the green. "Your cake made it through the night?"

"Yes it did," I called back. "I'll bring it over before judging starts."

I grabbed a hammer from my tool box and got to work. Around me, other vendors did the same—hammering, sawing, rebuilding. The sound of construction mixed with conversation and occasional laughter. It was one of the things I loved most about this town.

"Isla!" Amelia Avery appeared at my elbow, her husband Frank and daughter Amberlyn trailing behind. "Do you have a minute?"

I set down my hammer. "Of course. What's up?"

"We wanted to talk about the partnership." Amelia glanced at Frank, who nodded encouragingly. "Between our farm and your bakery. I know you've been busy, but we think it could be really special."

"I think so too." I wiped sawdust from my hands. "Your produce is perfect for what I do."

"That's what we were hoping." Amberlyn stepped forward, her phone already out. "I'm moving back to Acorn Field Heights, and I'd love to help you set up an online storefront. Expand your business beyond the physical bakery. You could take orders for shipping, do seasonal specials, maybe even wholesale to other local businesses."

My stomach dropped. "That sounds amazing, but I can't afford—"

"I'll do it for free." Amberlyn smiled. "It'll benefit my parents too if we're partnering. Besides, I'm investing in the valley now. Helping local businesses stay viable is part of that."

"Investing?" I glanced at Amelia, who was beaming.

"Amberlyn's putting money into several local operations," Frank explained. "Including yours, if you'll have it. Enough to hire help, upgrade equipment, expand your capacity."

"I—what?" My brain couldn't process what they were saying. "Why would you invest in my bakery?"

"Because it's good business," Amberlyn said matter-of-factly. "You make incredible baked goods, you have a loyal customer base, and with the right marketing and infrastructure, you could easily double your revenue. Maybe triple it within a year." She tapped her phone screen. "Once the online orders start coming in, you're going to need help. At least one full-time employee, maybe two."

Full-time employee. The words echoed in my head.

"Think about it," Amelia said gently. "We can talk details after the festival. But we wanted you to know we're serious about this partnership."

They walked away, leaving me standing in the wreckage of my booth with an idea taking root so fast I could barely breathe.

"You look like you've seen a ghost." Aunt Caroline appeared with her toolbox. "What did the Averys say?"

"They want to invest in the bakery. Help me expand." I stared at my half-rebuilt booth. "Amberlyn says I'll need to hire someone full-time."

"Well, that's wonderful!" Aunt Caroline started hammering a support beam into place. "About time you got some help again. You work yourself to death."

"Yeah." I grabbed my hammer, but my hands were shaking. "Yeah, it is."

We worked in silence for a while. By the time we finished, the booth looked almost normal. I brought out my competition cake and set it carefully on the display table.

Aunt Caroline whistled low. "That's gorgeous."

"Thank you." I adjusted the cake stand, making sure it caught the light just right. "Sawyer helped me finish it this morning."

"Did he now?"

"It's not like that. Maple ended up at the bakery last night, and Sawyer came looking for her." I wasn't sure how much Aunt Caroline knew, and I figured it was Sawyer's place to fill her in, not mine.

"Well, my nephew's got good hands if he can help with a competition cake." She leaned against the booth.

"Yeah," I smiled. "He could probably take my job someday if he wanted to." I paused, frowning. Take my job. Full-time employee. Stable work.

"Oh my—" I grabbed Aunt Caroline's arm. "What time is it?"

"Almost nine. Why?"

"I have to go." I was already moving, grabbing my keys from my bag. "But the baking competition—"

"I know!" I ran toward my car. "Cover for me!"

"Isla, what—"

But I was already in my car, engine roaring to life. The mediation started soon. Town Hall was five minutes away if I drove fast.

I drove very fast.

The Town Hall parking lot was nearly empty. I pulled in and killed the engine, my heart hammering against my ribs. What was I doing? This was crazy. I couldn't just walk into a custody mediation and—

Yes, I could. For Sawyer. For Maple.

I could do anything.

I pushed through the front doors and followed the sound of voices to a conference room at the end of the hall. Through the small window in the door, I could see Sawyer sitting at a table, Jen across from him, and a mediator between them. Maple sat next to a woman who must have been the guardian ad litem. There were a few other people scattered around the room.

The door was cracked, and as quietly as I could, I slipped and claimed a chair at the back of the room. Nobody even looked in my direction. The mediator continued speaking.

"—the issue remains that Mr. Thatcher has failed to secure stable employment." The mediator consulted his notes. "You've submitted applications to several positions, but none have resulted in offers. Is that correct?"

Sawyer's jaw was tight. "That's correct. But I'm still looking. I want to stay here with my daughter. She wants to stay here too."

"I do," Maple piped up, but she quickly closed her mouth when all the adults looked at her.

"I'm actively trying to look for a job. I promise." Sawyer said, tension radiating from his shoulders.

"No, he isn't." The words were out of my mouth before I could stop them. Every head in the room turned to look at me.

Sawyer's eyes went wide. "Isla?"

The mediator frowned. "I'm sorry, who are you?"

"Isla Mercado. I own Sugar & Spice Bakery on Main Street." I stood up, my legs shaking but my voice steady. "And I'm here to tell you that Sawyer isn't actively looking for work because he officially started working full-time at my bakery last night."

Silence. Complete, shocked silence.

"Full pay and benefits," I continued, walking toward the table. My eyes stayed locked on Sawyer's. "More than enough to support Maple. He's my new assistant baker and front-of-house manager. The position is permanent."

Sawyer stared at me like I'd grown a second head. "Isla, what are you—"

"Daddy works at the bakery?" Maple's excited voice cut through the confusion. "Really?"

I looked at her and smiled. "Really."

Maple launched herself out of her chair and ran straight at me. I caught her, lifting her up as she wrapped her arms around my neck. "Do I get to work too?"

"I do need someone to help come up with cookie designs," I whispered, holding her tight.

The mediator cleared his throat. "Ms. Mercado, this is highly irregular—"

"I can send you documentation after the festival when I get a chance to get on my computer." I adjusted my grip on Maple, who was still clinging to me. "I can send you the employment contract. Starting salary, benefits package, work schedule. Anything you need."

I didn't have documentation. I didn't have a contract. I didn't have anything except a desperate need to help the man I loved keep his daughter.

But I'd figure that out later.

Sawyer stood up slowly, his eyes shining. "You're serious."

"Completely serious." I set Maple down. "You helped me finish a competition cake at four in the morning after searching for your daughter all night. You follow instructions, you work hard, and Maple already loves spending time at the bakery. It's perfect."

"But you can't afford—"

"The Averys are investing. I can afford it." I looked at the mediator. "I can have all the paperwork to you by Monday. But Sawyer has stable employment as of last night. That's not going to change unless he wants to leave."

"I don't want to leave," he said, and I was pretty sure those words were just for me. "I never wanted to leave."

The mediator exchanged a glance with Jen's lawyer. "Do you have any objections to this development?"

Jen looked at Sawyer, then at Maple, then at me. Something complicated crossed her face—relief, maybe, or resignation. "No. No objections."

"Then I think we can proceed with joint custody discussions," the mediator said. "Mr. Thatcher, it appears you've addressed the court's primary concern about stability."

Sawyer's legs seemed to give out. He sank back into his chair, his head in his hands. His shoulders shook, and I realized he was crying again. But this time it was relief, not fear.

Maple climbed into his lap, patting his face. "Don't cry, Daddy. You got a job! At the bakery! With Miss Isla!"

He pulled her close, pressing his face into her hair. "Yeah, baby. I did."

I stepped back, giving them space. The mediator was already shuffling papers, talking about custody schedules and holiday arrangements. Jen was nodding, her lawyer taking notes.

I slipped toward the door, but Sawyer's voice stopped me.

"Isla. Wait."

I turned. He was standing now, Maple on his hip, his eyes red but clear.

"Thank you," he said. "I don't know how I'll ever—"

"You can start by showing up for your first official shift tomorrow." I smiled at him. "Six a.m. Don't be late."

"I won't." He shifted Maple to his other hip. "I love you."

"I love you too." I glanced at the mediator, who was pointedly not looking at us. "Now finish this meeting so you can come watch me lose the baking competition."

"You're not going to lose."

"I left my cake unattended at the festival grounds. It's probably been eaten by birds by now."

I left before he could respond, pushing back out into the October sunshine. My hands were shaking. My heart was racing. I'd just offered someone a full-time job I couldn't afford three hours ago, walked into a custody mediation I had no business being in, and possibly ruined my chance at winning the baking competition.

But Sawyer had his daughter. That was all that mattered.

Chapter Fifteen

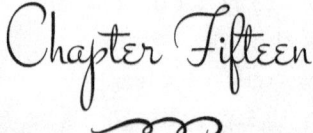

SAWYER

"Did we miss it?" I asked Isla as Maple and I found her in the cloud of people.

"No," Isla said, her attention wholly fixed on the small stage.

"Good." We'd made it back to the festival just as Mayor Goldwin was re-announcing the competition winners—his microphone apparently fixed.

"As I was saying before technical difficulties," he boomed, "first place in our annual baking competition goes to Margaret Morrison for her spectacular five-tier autumn cake!"

My heart sank. Isla had worked so hard, stayed up all night perfecting her entry despite everything else falling apart around us. She squeezed my hand and smiled, but I could see the disappointment she was trying to hide.

"The two thousand dollar second place prize goes to Isla Mercado!" Mayor Goldwin continued.

Beside me, Isla smiled as she made her way up to accept her ribbon.

People applauded. Maple, who'd been remarkably well-behaved during the mediation aftermath, now jumped up and down shrieking, "Miss Isla won! She won something!"

"Yes she did," I murmured beaming at Isla as she flushed from all the attention.

She made her way back through the crowd, ribbon in hand and cheeks pink. Maple launched herself at Isla before she'd fully descended the stage steps.

"You won! You won!" Maple wrapped her arms around Isla's legs. "Can I have cake now?"

"Maybe after lunch. That's up you your dad," Isla said, ruffling her hair. She looked up at me, and something soft crossed her face. "Thanks for coming."

"Wouldn't have missed it." I pulled her close with my free arm, Maple squished between us. "Second place is amazing. That cake was perfect."

"It wasn't perfect. The cream cheese frosting was slightly too soft on the left side, and I should have let the layers cool another five minutes before assembly." She sighed. "Margaret's cake really was spectacular though. Five tiers? That takes serious skill."

"Next year we'll win first," I said.

"Oh yeah?" Her eyebrow arched.

"I'm your assistant baker now, remember? That means I'm invested in our competition strategy." I grinned at her. "Besides, I have a whole year to watch all the Youtube tutorials I can. And I helped make your cake. I want my revenge on Margaret Morrison. We're a team now. Next year, first place. I'm thinking we go bigger—maybe six tiers. Really show Margaret what we're made of."

"Six tiers would require structural support and—" She stopped, catching my expression. "You're already planning this, aren't you?"

"I've got a whole year to learn from the best baker in Acorn Field Heights." I squeezed her hand. "We're going to crush it."

"We," she repeated, like she was testing the word. Then she smiled, wide and real. "Yeah. We are."

Maple tugged on both our hands. "Can we go see the pumpkins now? And the goats? Daddy, you promised I could feed the goats!"

"I did promise that." I glanced at Isla. "Want to come with us? We could grab lunch at Aunt Caroline's booth after."

"I'd love to." She laced her fingers through mine, and Maple grabbed her other hand, creating a chain between the three of us.

We walked through the festival like that, Maple swinging between us and chattering about everything she saw. The storm damage was barely visible now—the community had pulled together and rebuilt what mattered. Booths stood straight, banners flew bright, and people laughed and ate and celebrated the harvest despite everything.

Near the costume contest booth, I spotted my youngest brother Asher standing close to Quinn, his hand hovering near her lower back. Quinn was laughing at something he'd said, her whole face lit up.

"Your brother's got it bad," Isla murmured, following my gaze.

"Yeah, he does." I watched Asher finally work up the courage to put his arm around Quinn's shoulders, watched her lean into him without hesitation. "Good for him. He deserves something good."

"They both do." Isla squeezed my hand. "Speaking of deserving good things—how did the rest of mediation go?"

"Joint custody. She'll have weekends, the summer, and most holidays with Jen, but the school year she'll be here. They liked the kindergarten, I think." My throat tightened remembering Jen's face when the mediator announced the terms. "Jen wasn't happy about it, but she agreed. Said she wants what's best for Maple."

"And what's best for Maple is having both her parents." Isla stopped walking, turning to face me fully. "You did it, Sawyer. You fought for her and you won."

"We won." I pulled her close, resting my forehead against hers. "I couldn't have done any of this without you."

"Oh, look there are the goats!" Maple tugged on our hands. "Can we please go see the goats now?"

Isla laughed. "Come on. Let's go feed some goats before your daughter stages a rebellion."

We walked toward the petting zoo area, Maple practically dragging us along. The October sun was warm on my shoulders, the air smelled like cider and cinnamon.

Six months ago, I'd been terrified and alone, barely keeping my head above water as Jen's custody threats closed in around me. Three months ago, I'd come home to Acorn Field Heights with nothing but hope and a five-year-old who deserved better than I'd been giving her.

And now? Now I had a job I was excited about, a woman I loved who loved me back, and a daughter who was safe and happy. Now I had a future that looked like something I actually wanted instead of something I was just trying to survive.

"Daddy, look!" Maple pointed at the goat pen where several kids were climbing on everything in sight. "Can I go in?"

"Go ahead. We'll watch from here."

She ran off, immediately befriending a small brown goat that looked as energetic as she was. Isla leaned against the fence beside me, her shoulder warm against mine.

"Thank you," I whispered. "For the job. For showing up at mediation. For—" I gestured vaguely at everything. "All of it."

"You would've figured something out." She turned to look at me. "But I'm glad I could help. And I meant what I said—I need someone at the bakery. This isn't charity, Sawyer. You're going to earn every penny."

"Six a.m. tomorrow morning. I'll be there."

"With coffee. Don't forget the coffee."

"I would never." I kissed her, soft and quick. "I love you."

"I love you too." She rested her head on my shoulder. "Now let's make a bet."

"A bet?"

"Who's going to be terrorized more? The goats or the volunteer watching your daughter chase the goats?"

"Definitely the volunteer," I said, grinning.

We stood there together, watching Maple laugh and play in the October sunshine, and for the first time in longer than I could remember, everything felt exactly right.

Read the First Chapter in Asher and Quinn's Book

Chapter 1

QUINN

I was overdressed, and everyone knew it. The velvet blazer that made me feel like a creative professional in the city made me look like I'd wandered off a period drama set here in Acorn Field Heights, where flannel was apparently formal wear. Twenty faces turned toward me as I stepped into the town hall basement, and I could feel them staring at every vintage button on my plum-colored jacket.

The flannel-to-velvet ratio in this room was approximately 20:1, and I was the one.

I chose a seat in the back row, setting my portfolio on my knees and trying to look like someone who belonged. The basement smelled like burnt coffee and fifty years of committee meetings, with fluorescent lights that made everyone look vaguely ill. Old wiring snaked across the ceiling—exposed cloth insulation in places, the kind that made fire marshals nervous. Metal folding chairs scraped against linoleum as people settled in.

My phone buzzed in my pocket. Fifteen percent battery, even though I'd charged it this morning. The thing was dying a slow death, but between rent and inventory costs and keeping Enchanted Threads afloat these past three months, a new phone wasn't exactly priority spending.

My gaze drifted across the room when it snagged on the guy in the corner.

He sat apart from everyone else, one ankle crossed over his knee, a worn notebook balanced on his thigh. Dark hair fell across his forehead as he bent over the page. Even from fifteen feet away I could see his pencil moving in quick strokes. He wore a dark green flannel shirt rolled to his elbows, revealing forearms marked by thin white scars—the kind that came from working with tools or climbing trees as a kid.

His hands moved across the page. Long fingers, callused at the tips. I watched one hand shift his pencil grip while the other braced the notebook. My pulse jumped for a second, watching how intently focused he was on the page. Paint stains marked his jeans—forest green and burnt umber on the left knee, like he'd been mixing autumn colors. A smear of titanium white on his right thigh.

He glanced up. His gaze met mine across the room—gray-green, like sea glass. My breath caught. Then he was back to his notebook, but heat climbed up my neck.

"You must be Quinn."

I jumped. A woman with silver hair and a kind smile stood next to my chair, holding a clipboard.

"Caroline Thatcher, but everyone calls me Aunt Caroline. I run Harvest Moon Café." She handed me a paper cup of coffee that looked strong enough to wake the dead. "Welcome to town."

"Thank you." I accepted the coffee, wrapping my hands around it. "Still finding my way around."

"Three months is hardly enough time to settle in, but you're doing wonderfully." She smiled. "Your shop is lovely."

Before I could respond, a man in his sixties clapped his hands twice.

"Alright, everyone. Let's get started." Mayor Goldwin consulted his clipboard. "We are just three weeks out from the fall festival. That means we're behind schedule and need all hands on deck."

Mayor Goldwin worked through his agenda. Booth assignments, parking logistics, corn maze updates. I tried to focus, but my attention kept drifting to Corner Guy. His pencil never stopped moving.

"Quinn Fairchild opened Enchanted Threads on Main Street back in July," Mayor Goldwin said. "Quinn, would you like to tell us about your booth idea?"

Every head swiveled toward me.

I stood, smoothing my blazer with damp palms. "Hi, everyone. Thank you for letting me participate." I opened my portfolio. "I was thinking we could set up a Halloween costume photo booth. Professional backdrop, vintage props, some pieces from my shop that people could borrow for photos."

Silence. Someone coughed.

"Families love this kind of thing," I continued, talking too fast. "It creates shareable content for social media, which helps promote the festival—"

"What kind of costumes?" a woman near the front interrupted.

"Sorry?"

"What kind of costumes would people borrow? My kids are picky."

Relief flooded through me. "Everything from authentic Victorian— I have an 1880s bustle gown with original jet beading—to 1920s flapper dresses. For kids, I've got pirates with real brass buckles, a whole collection of 1950s poodle skirts. All professionally cleaned, all historically accurate."

"I love it," someone else said.

"Me too," another voice added. "The social media aspect is brilliant!" The young woman who spoke seemed to be about my age, and she sat with her phone in her hands.

"Thanks." I relaxed a bit. "I was also thinking quick costume consultations. Help people put together looks using pieces they already own, plus maybe one or two rental items. Make it accessible for families on a budget."

A sharp snap made me lose my train of thought. The artist guy's pencil tip broke against his notebook. He didn't look up, just reached into his shirt pocket for another pencil.

"Sounds perfect," Mayor Goldwin said. "We'll put you near the gazebo." He scanned the room. "You'll need help with setup. Asher Thatcher, you've got an artistic eye. You'll work with Quinn on this."

The pencil went still.

Asher—so that was his name—looked up. His eyes met mine, and I registered the same gray-green from before. Something careful lived in that gaze, like he was already calculating distance.

"Sure," he said. His voice was low, rough around the edges. "I'll text you."

That was it. He was already back to his notebook before Mayor Goldwin moved on.

The meeting continued for another thirty minutes, but I'd lost the thread. My phone buzzed in my pocket—probably Carter again. He'd been calling more frequently lately, leaving messages about "reconnecting" that made my skin crawl. I'd stopped answering two months ago, but he'd never been good at respecting boundaries.

When Mayor Goldwin finally adjourned, I gathered my portfolio. Several people smiled at me as they passed. I turned to find Asher already halfway to the door.

My feet moved before my brain caught up. I squeezed through the crowd and caught him just as he pushed open the exit door.

"Hey," I called.

He stopped, one hand on the door, and turned back. Up close, I could see he was probably late twenties, with sharp cheekbones and a small scar cutting through his left eyebrow. Paint stains dotted his flannel.

"I'm Quinn. I guess we're working together?"

"Looks that way."

I waited. He didn't add anything.

The silence stretched awkwardly. I fumbled with my portfolio, and the clasp popped open. Papers exploded everywhere—sketches, fabric samples, vendor contacts scattering across the floor.

"Perfect," I muttered, dropping to my knees.

Asher crouched down at the same moment. We nearly collided, heads missing by inches. His hand landed on top of mine as we both reached for the same sketch. For a heartbeat we froze there, too close, his gray-green eyes meeting mine with an intensity that stole my breath.

Then he pulled back, gathering papers. His gaze caught on one of my inventory lists. "You've got good organization. Organized by era?"

"Makes it easier to track rentals." My voice came out breathier than intended. "And repairs."

He handed me the stack, fingers brushing mine. "Smart."

It was the first real thing he'd said to me, and I stared like he'd just recited poetry.

"So maybe we should meet this week?" I stood, shoving papers back into my portfolio. "Go over the design—"

"I'll text you." He was already turning away.

"Right, but when?" I pulled out a business card—cream with purple script—and held it out.

He took it without really looking, shoving it into his back pocket. "I'll be in touch."

Then he was gone.

I stood there, papers still half-hanging out, watching through the door's small window as he crossed to a beat-up truck. He moved with his shoulders hunched against the wind.

"Don't mind Asher."

I turned to find Aunt Caroline beside me.

"He's a good kid. Just needs time to warm up. He's the youngest of his brothers, my nephews. He'll be perfect for you."

"Excuse me?"

"I mean, he's become the town's handyman since he returned home from college. He'll be the perfect match for you." She paused with a suspicious smirk. "And your booth."

"Of course." I forced a smile.

Aunt Caroline patted my arm and headed back inside.

I pushed open the door. The October air bit through my blazer. The village green stretched dark ahead of me. In three weeks this space would be full of booths and families.

If I was still here. If I hadn't already failed at fitting in.

My car sat two blocks down. I walked past the hardware store, past Harvest Moon Café with its cinnamon-scented air, past the closed bakery. And then I saw it.

Enchanted Threads.

My shop. My sign in gold and purple script. Through the window I could see the vintage mannequins, the costume racks, the Victorian fainting couch I'd reupholstered.

I'd built this. After Carter and his control issues and the slow erosion of my sense of self, I'd packed up my life and started over. Three months of fourteen-hour days and mounting debt, but I'd built this.

A man who couldn't say more than five words didn't change that.

I unlocked my car and slid in, tossing my portfolio onto the passenger seat. Something tumbled off and landed in my lap—a worn notebook with a leather cover.

My breath caught.

Asher's notebook.

I must've grabbed it when he was helping me pick up my papers. It'd been an accident, of course. I knew I should leave it alone. But my fingers seemed to have a mind of their own since they were already opening the cover.

The first page held a detailed sketch of the town square, every architectural detail drawn with care. I turned the page. It was a sunrise—or sunset, I couldn't be sure—with a barn in the foreground and a horse running in a pasture. The next page showed more landscape sketches, then a portrait of an elderly woman, then Main Street storefronts.

And then I found it.

"Festival booth" written at the top in sharp handwriting. Below it, rough concept sketches—a backdrop with autumn leaves, prop placement, a floor plan. Notes in the margins: "Lighting important," "Vintage camera on tripod?" "Check about color scheme."

My throat went tight.

He'd been paying attention. Listening to my pitch and sketching ideas while I talked.

My phone buzzed. Unknown number.

> This is Asher Thatcher. Saturday 9am, your shop. I'll bring preliminary sketches.

I stared at the text a few seconds longer than necessary before responding.

> Sounds good. See you then.

I hit send, then added another message.

> BTW, You left your notebook at the meeting.
> I have it if you need it before Saturday.

Three dots appeared. Disappeared. Appeared again.

> Keep it until Saturday. I'll get it back then.

I tucked the notebook into my portfolio and started my car. The drive to my rental cottage took three minutes.

Inside, I made tea and changed into sweats and wrapped up my frizzy orange hair into the messiest of buns.

It didn't take long before I was thinking about him. About the contradiction between his distance and his sketches. About the way his pencil had moved with the same focused attention I'd seen in his eyes. About those paint stains that made me think he created things with hands that knew how to be gentle and sure.

I fell asleep with his notebook on my nightstand.

Read the rest of Asher and Quinn's
story in the next book...

Secret Kisses & Twilight Wishes

Make Sure To Check Out All 3 Cute Fall Romcoms With The Thatcher Brothers!

Make Sure To Check Out Maggie Ellis's First Christmas Novella

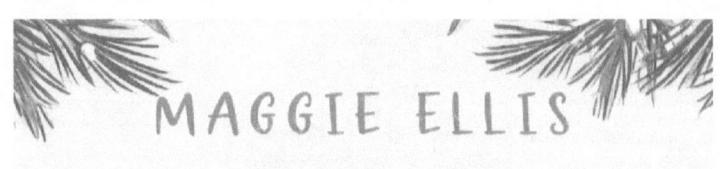

MAGGIE ELLIS

The Christmas Cabin Mix-Up

A CUTE HOLIDAY NOVELLA

Acknowledgments

To my husband. Thank you for making sure I'm never without snacks, water, or encouragement. You're my calm in every deadline storm and my favorite chapter of every story.

To my wonderful beta readers, Rachel H., Becca L., and Jenn C.—you made this book stronger, sweeter, and so much more fun. Your insights, laughter, and enthusiasm kept me going when the words got tangled. I'm endlessly thankful for you.

To my four-legged writing assistant, who insists on being involved in every scene (preferably from my lap). Thank you for your patience, snuggles, and occasional edits in the form of paw prints.

And to you, dear reader. Thank you for coming back to Acorn Field Heights and falling in love with these characters right alongside me. I hope this story makes you laugh, sigh, and believe in second chances. May your candles burn bright, your cocoa stay hot, and your heart feel right at home.

With love,
Maggie

IF YOU ENJOYED THIS SWEET FALL ROMCOM, PLEASE CONSIDER LEAVING A REVIEW. IT HELPS OUT A TON!

About the Author

Maggie Ellis writes swoony, clean romantic comedies filled with awkward meet-cutes, heartfelt moments, and more than a few cups of coffee. When she's not dreaming up cute romances, she can usually be found baking something unnecessarily complicated, wandering through independent bookstores, or losing another sock to the dryer gremlins. She lives in a small town where everyone waves and the Wi-Fi is questionable, but the inspiration is endless.